Cesare Pavese

The Leucothea Dialogues

Translated from the Italian by Minna Zallman Proctor

archipelago books

First Archipelago Books Edition, 2025

Library of Congress Cataloging-in-Publication Data available upon request.

ISBN: 978-1-962770-37-8

Archipelago Books
232 3rd Street #A111
Brooklyn, NY 11215
WWW.ARCHIPELAGOBOOKS.ORG

Cover art: Kupferstich-Kabinett, Staatliche Kunstsammlungen Dresden
Photo: Andreas Diesend

The quotation on pages 15-16 was taken from *Family Lexicon* by Natalia Ginzburg, translated by Jenny McPhee, New York Review Books Classics, 2017. The quotation on page 20 was taken from Italo Calvino's "Ovid and Universal Contiguity" in *The Uses of Literature*, translated by Patrick Creagh, Harcourt Brace Jovanovich, 1987.

The authorized representative in the EU for product safety and compliance is eucomply OÜ, Pärnu mnt 139b-14, 11317 Tallinn, Estonia, HELLO@EUCOMPLIANCEPARTNER.COM, +33 757690241

This work is made possible by the New York State Council on the Arts with the support of the Office of the Governor and the New York State Legislature.

This publication was made possible with support from the Hawthornden Foundation, the Carl Lesnor Family Foundation, the National Endowment for the Arts, and the New York City Department of Cultural Affairs.

This book was translated thanks to a grant awarded by the Italian Ministry of Foreign Affairs and International Cooperation.

PRINTED IN CANADA

The Leucothea Dialogues

I need myths, fantastical and universal, to fully and unforgettably express this experience that is my place in the world.

—Cesare Pavese, from a letter to Fernanda Pivano,
June 27, 1942

Table of Contents

THE INTRODUCTION THAT FOLLOWS IS NARRATED BY ARACHNE, ON BEHALF OF THE TRANSLATOR. Before relinquishing the stage, the translator would like to acknowledge that the author and many characters in this book died by suicide. There is biographical evidence substantial enough to support one interpretation of this complex work as, if not a preamble to the Author's suicide note, then at least a detailed philosophical exploration of the meaning of life and death—with human mortality and divine immortality as inextricably twinned embodiments of the debate. Because the Author wrote his last words on the title page of this book and set it beside him on the nightstand of the otherwise empty and anonymous hotel room in which he took his life, it is difficult not to assume that he meant this book, too, to represent his last words. What's more, just days before his death the Author wrote in a letter to a dear friend: "If you want to know who I am now, reread 'Beast' from my dialogues."

"Beast" is the story of young Endymion who was imprisoned by Artemis in a perpetual sleep, because she thought him pretty. He's exhausted, deranged, and frustrated by Artemis's refusal to smile at him the way she did when they first met: "If she would only smile again, I would bleed for her, be the flesh in her dog's mouth." Tortured by the goddess's unkind love, Endymion asks, "Have you ever known someone who was many things at once, who contained all—every gesture, every thought you've had about her—who holds vast things from your world, your sky, and your words, memories, days past you'll never know, future days, everything you're sure of, and another world, another sky that you can't have?" He continues, "What if she were the beast, the wild thing, the untouchable nature that has no name?"

But who really is the Beast in this equation? The goddess with her fierce incomprehensible passions or the trapped, sleepless youth driven mad with love? Who is the animal? Who is the "wild thing"? And who is the Author, hunter or prey?

The great Sicilian writer Leonardo Sciascia said, "A man who dies tragically is, at any moment of his life, a man who will die tragically." The end colors everything that precedes it. There is an irresistible invitation to speculate, and yet, there is also something sordid about trying to find an explanation for personal tragedy in a work of literature, even one that vastly contemplates life and death. In the years after Pavese's suicide, Natalia Ginzburg, another of the Author's closest friends, resisted the urge to pitch an explanation and instead made this observation:

> He didn't have any specific motive for killing himself. However, he'd assembled a variety of motives, adding them up with lightning precision, combining them this way and that, proving to himself that from any angle the result was the same and therefore definitive, a decision he confirmed with that wicked smile. He also gazed beyond his own life into the future to see how people would behave with respect to his books and his memory.

Like those who love life and don't know how to detach themselves from it, he looked beyond death and imagined death to the point where it was no longer death he imagined but life. In any case, he didn't love life, and his gaze beyond his own death was not driven by love of life but rather a shrewd calculation of circumstances so that nothing, even after he was dead, could take him by surprise.

TRANSLATOR'S INTRODUCTION IN ONE ACT

Arachne enters center stage, emerging into the spotlight from total darkness. She takes a seat on a plain wooden stool. She looks uncomfortable, and then stands again. She will disdain the stool for the entirety of her monologue.

ARACHNE:

Here's the story . . . This is a story about a translation of the book, *Dialoghi con Leucò*, a story I have to tell, because the translator [*gestures vaguely to the wings*] is so exhausted, she couldn't bear to explain one thing more. But if you ask me, she couldn't bear to understand one thing more. It is an unusual book.

Here's the story: Cesare, ch-ey-SAH-ray, Pavese, pah-VEY-sey, was an Italian poet, novelist, and translator. He is a great hero for figures like me, who don't exist without people to write about them. I would have thought I'd be a hero to him too, as a story weaver myself and all. You'd think I was a hero to him, but he never wrote about me so . . . So so so sew. So that makes me the perfect choice to introduce him. I am unbiased [*makes a snorting sound, pauses for laughter*]. As you all know, "without bias" is a myth.

Mostly Pavese wrote poems and novels about very ordinary things, about cats and young women, unattainable love, village life, death, and about the war—because that's what was going on in Europe in the nineteen thirties and nineteen forties when he was writing. Some say his most important work was his debut poetry collection, *Work's Tiring*; others claim it was his last novel, *The Moon and the Bonfires*, which was published in 1949, the year before he died at only forty-two years old. No one ever claims his most important work was a peculiar little collection of twenty-seven lyrical dialogues featuring the gods and heroes of ancient Greece, *Dialoghi con Leucò* . . . Hold on—parenthesis.

(That title literally translates as "dialogues with Leucò," where Leucò is short for Leucothea, the sea nymph whose name was Ino when she was mortal, before she threw herself off a cliff with her baby son in her arms to escape the curse of insanity that Hera had put on her. Sometimes she's referred to as the White Goddess. People, especially women, are always throwing themselves off cliffs in Greek tragedy and mythology. Though that's not how I went, and that's not how Cesare Pavese went.)

It's probably also important to parenthetically mention that the translator is proposing an entirely different title. She likes changing titles and always has excellent and long-winded reasoning to justify it. Nothing I'll bore you with. She calls the book *The Leucothea Dialogues*. [*Shrugs.*] I guess that sort of makes sense even without a tiresome, self-important justification. That said, this translated title doesn't really accurately represent the original title, and when you start changing things like that, someone might complain that you're challenging the real author—like you're saying to them,

"Hey, you know how you titled your book in this slightly obscure way, using the nickname of a slightly obscure goddess? Well, I have a better idea."

I've "heard" that comparing yourself to gods can make them mad. And for a translator the dead author is a kind of god—the unreachable, singular intelligence who created the world that you're supposed to re-communicate in a whole new language? But then again, although Pavese acted like a god—all writers do—he wasn't really an immortal, otherwise he'd be here fighting his own battles.

I'd say he's more of a myth, an immortal myth.

Looks at invisible person sitting on the stool and grins.

You see how I just brought things back around to mythology?

Turns attention back to the audience.

As I was saying, no one ever claims that these dialogues were Pavese's most important book. When the book came out in Italy, there were hardly any reviews or letters from colleagues eager to discuss. He was terribly disappointed, but also perversely pleased. In a letter to a friend, he wrote, "No one dares speculate about the meaning of my book—and that delights me to no end." To one of his unrequited loves, he wrote, "I want you to understand it, and it's a bitter thrill that you don't."

But all these years later, seventy-five years later in fact, people still can't shut up about these dialogues. They're "unreadable." They're "difficult." They're "allegories." They're "autobiography." They're "a suicide note." They're "a mystery." So many theories and academic papers and doctoral dissertations and unresolved Reddit forums . . . [*Yawns.*] Look, Italo Calvino wrote that "a classic is a book that has never finished saying what it has to say." Which maybe sums up what's happening here. It does strike me, however, that all Reddit forums are essentially unresolved.

Either way, there's this important, complicated book by a dead white European man and everyone with a robust tolerance for dead white European men is either fascinated by it, or repelled by it, or [*shrugs*] I guess maybe hasn't heard of it.

So, the Italians said to the translator, "These dialogues are so incomprehensible, hermetic, intentionally difficult . . . We can't even understand them in Italian, how will you translate them?" Maybe there's also the implied question, "*Why* will you translate them?"

I can tell you [*lowers voice and leans forward to share a secret*] she didn't really have an answer. Not a rational one, anyway.

Translation is a world of pain . . . You have to understand what you're translating—or what comes out is second-degree gibberish—and this text doesn't give itself away. That's why she's off resting [*nods toward the wings again*]. You can't translate incomprehension or ambiguity, secret references, private symbols, invented idioms. You have to parse and then re-create. Create it all over, as if from scratch, as if you were the author—as if you could ever inhabit the mind of another person. The hubris.

She disengages. Turns her back to the audience for a moment, then walks in a dreamy circle around the stool, coming back to face front, a refreshed expression on her face.

I keep thinking about that "wicked smile" from the Natalia Ginzburg quote. He didn't have any particular motive for killing himself. However, he'd put together various motives, adding them—combining them—proving to himself that from any angle the result was the same and definitive, a decision he confirmed with his wicked smile. Do you know that smiling appears forty-four times in this book? And in none of those occurrences does it ever have to do with a joke or joy. It is a wicked smile. It has divine properties. The gods smile and marvel to each other about how none of the mortals know how to smile. I think that this wicked god-smile has to do with knowing—knowing something so definitively, so fully and absolutely, that you have no choice but to accept it. You know and understand and accept it all because that's just how it is. [*She smiles broadly.*]

On the topic of Italo Calvino, let's talk about me for a minute. Since Pavese didn't. [*Pauses thoughtfully.*]

Do you think Pavese was jealous of me? I am quite a renowned storyteller. [*Makes weaving motions in the air above her head like a spider.*]

Either way, let's take me as an example. According to my biographer Ovid [*swooning a little and fanning herself*], in my looming contest with Athena, I wove stories of the gods doing their basest, most criminal things—all that raping and deception, jealousy and impatience. Whereas she loomed stories of the gods viciously punishing mortals who challenged them. Got it? She was trying to induce holy terror. I was inciting people to irreverence and moral relativism. At least, this is how Italo Calvino breaks it down in his critical commentary on my biographer.

Calvino says it's a mistake to think that because Athena gets so mad about me beating her in the weaving contest that Ovid is telling a story about

Athena's absolute power. And it's also a mistake to think that Ovid is casting me, little old me, as a hero, just because, obviously, I'm the more sympathetic figure. I also think it's confusing in terms of moral coding, because I was, strictly speaking, a suicide. True, I was driven to suicide by Athena's wrath. But in the last moment, she saved me. She took pity on me. An ambiguous salvation . . . to be turned into an immortal spider.

[*Assumes a flirtatious pose.*] I look pretty good for an old spider, though, right?

Bear with me, this is what Calvino says about Ovid, and about gods and mythology: [*takes out a notebook and puts on her reading glasses if she isn't already wearing them*]

> Ovid's *Metamorphoses* aims to represent all that is worth telling of what has been passed down by literature, and with all the force of images and meanings that this implies, without deciding between the various keys in which it can be read—in accord with the ambiguity that is proper to myth. Only by giving a place in the poem to all the stories or implied stories that flow in every direction, that push and shove to channel themselves into the well-ordered expanses of his hexameters, can the author of the Metamorphoses be sure of presenting no partial design, but rather a living multiplicity that excludes no god known or unknown.

That's very generous of him. [*Puts away notebook.*] A living multiplicity that excludes no god . . . Gives a place to all the stories and implied stories. That's the kind of book that can't finish saying what it has to say.

She hangs her head and grows very still. After a moment, she quietly continues.

Suicide is ambiguous. The person who dies leaves their pain behind for everyone else to deal with. [*Shakes head.*] But I don't think Pavese really thought he was escaping anything when he took his own life. Because all the mortals in his book are disappointed in their afterlife. And all the immortals in the book are terribly emphatic that mortality itself is a precious gift, the one thing humans have that the gods don't. They're always complaining about how humans have the unique capacity to value their fleeting existence, the moments past, the moments to come. Pavese's gods get very angry when the humans take that for granted. You see, it's ambiguous, and the ambiguity isn't vague, it's faceted, it's a living multiplicity!

Why did Pavese leave his odd, cryptic suicide note ("I forgive everyone and ask everyone's forgiveness. OK? Don't gossip too much.") on the title page of *this* book and place it on the nightstand beside him in the anonymous hotel room where he took his own life?

During the final few moments of the monologue, the stage has been growing darker, and the spotlight on Arachne more intense. She is practically a floating white face, cut with fierce shadows that make her look even more like a spider.

I think it's because he didn't want resolution. Like Ovid, he wanted to contain all the stories he'd told and the ones those stories implied, a living multiplicity that extended far beyond his own self.

The spotlight extinguishes. Arachne delivers her last line in complete darkness.

He never wanted to finish . . .

AUTHOR'S FOREWORD

Given the choice, a person could certainly get by with less mythology. But we've come to accept mythology as a language, an expressive mode—which is to say, it's not random, it's a hothouse of symbols that belongs, like all languages do, to a specific set of references that can't be conveyed any other way. When we repeat a proper noun, an action, a mythical feat, we are expressing—in short, with simplicity—a synthetic and comprehensive fact, a kernel of reality that brings to life and nurtures an entire organism of passion, of the human condition, the entirety of a conceptual framework. If the noun or gesture reminds us of childhood or our schooldays, all the better. Disquiet is more real and pointed when stirring up the familiar. What's immediate and conventional about the Greek myths, how understandably popular they are, is adequate for us. We're so frightened of the irregular, abnormal, or coincidental, and we go to great, even physical, lengths to establish limits and perimeters—to make sure whatever it is will be over and done with. We've grown convinced that great revelations can only be drawn from the stubborn rehashing of the same problems. We're nothing like world travelers, inventors, or adventurers. We know that the best and quickest path to surprise is to stare fearlessly and steadily at the same object. Then—there is that perfect moment when, miracle of miracles, that same object will seem like something we've never seen before.

THE CLOUD

Ixion & Nephele

That Ixion's audacity landed him in Tartarus is likely. It's unlikely though that he spawned Centaurs from a cloud. There was already a nation of Centaurs before the wedding of Ixion's son. The Lapiths and Centaurs come from the time of the Titans when beings of all kinds mingled freely, and the monster proliferation was beaten down by Olympus's merciless attacks.

THE CLOUD That's the law, Ixion. Laws must be obeyed.

IXION The law doesn't apply up here, Nephele. Up here, the law is a blizzard, a storm, it's the darkness. And when the sky clears and you float alongside this peak, it's too beautiful to think of anything else.

THE CLOUD There is law, Ixion, now like never before. It's a stronger fist gathering the clouds.

IXION That fist can't reach us here. The weather's clear now and even you are laughing. But when the sky darkens and the winds shriek, who will care about that hand tap-tapping like raindrops? Those things already happened before the masters came. Nothing changes on mountaintops. This is what we're used to.

THE CLOUD Lots of things changed on the mountaintops. Look at Mount Pelion, look at Mount Ossa and Olympus. Even the more remote mountains.

IXION So, what's changed on the mountains, Nephele?

THE CLOUD Not the sun or the water, Ixion. What's changed is the fate of mankind. There are monsters now. Mankind is limited. Water, wind, the cliffs, and clouds are no longer yours. You don't get to cling to them, breeding and living. The world is held in other hands now. There is law, Ixion.

IXION What law?

THE CLOUD You already know. Your fate, your limitations . . .

IXION My fate is in my own hands, Nephele. What's changed? Are these new lords going to stop me from throwing boulders for fun, or from going into the valley to break my enemy's back? Will they be worse than exhaustion and death?

THE CLOUD That's not it, Ixion. You can do all of that and more. But you can't mingle with us anymore, the nymphs of the mountains and the streams, the daughters of the wind, the earth goddesses. Destiny has changed.

IXION What do you mean *anymore*?

THE CLOUD I mean that you'll intend to do one thing and will do something horrible instead. Like the man who goes to hug a friend but strangles him or gets strangled.

IXION I don't understand. So, you won't come to the mountain anymore? Are you scared of me?

THE CLOUD I'll come to the mountain and go wherever I want. But you can't do anything to me, Ixion. You can't do anything about the water or wind. Instead, you must bow down. That's your only chance.

IXION You're scared, Nephele.

THE CLOUD I am scared. I've seen the tops of mountains. But I'm not scared for myself, Ixion. I can't suffer. I'm frightened for you because you're only men. As ruler, you used to run these mountains—and these beings, our creations, who were born in freedom will now tremble at the slightest gesture. We're all indentured to a stronger hand. Centaurs, the children of water and wind, the Centaurs are all hiding in caves. They know they're monsters.

IXION Who says?

THE CLOUD Don't challenge the hand, Ixion. It is fate. I have seen those who are more audacious than you, or them, tumble from the cliffs and not die. Listen to me, Ixion. Death, which was your courage, can be taken from you as if it were property. Don't you know this?

IXION You've told me that before. It doesn't matter. We'll just live bigger.

THE CLOUD You joke, but you don't know the immortals.

IXION I'd like to meet them.

THE CLOUD But Ixion, you're imagining presences like us—like Night, Earth, or old Pan. You're young, Ixion, but you were born under the old destiny. You don't think in terms of monsters, you think about friends. Death, you think, is a thing that happens, like night or day. You are one of us, Ixion. You are what you do. But to them, to the immortals, what you do has meaning that extends. They palpate everything from a great distance—with their eyes, noses, lips. They are immortal and don't know how to live alone. Whatever you achieve or can't achieve, whatever you say or seek—it's all for their pleasure or displeasure. And if you offend them, accidentally disrupt them in their Olympus, they'll come down on you, bring you death—their version of death, a death that lingers as a bitter taste and feeling.

IXION So it is still possible to die.

THE CLOUD No, Ixion. They'll make a shadow of you—a shadow that wants life back but never dies.

IXION You've seen these gods?

THE CLOUD I've seen them . . . . Oh, Ixion, you don't know what you're asking.

IXION Well, I've seen them too, Nephele. And they aren't so terrible.

THE CLOUD I knew it. Your fate is sealed. Who did you see?

IXION Who knows? A young man walking barefoot through the forest. He passed near me but didn't say a word. Then he disappeared in front of a cliff. I spent a long time looking for him, to ask him who he was—I was so struck. He seemed made of the same flesh as you.

THE CLOUD That's the only one you saw?

IXION Then I saw him again in a dream—with the goddesses. And I felt like I belonged among them, talking and laughing. They were telling me all the same things you've been saying, but fearlessly, not trembling as you are. We all talked about destiny and death. We spoke of Olympus and laughed about all the silly monsters . . .

THE CLOUD Oh Ixion, Ixion, your fate is sealed. And now you know what's changed on the mountaintops. And that has changed you. Now you think that you are somehow more than a man.

IXION I'm telling you, Nephele, they're just like you. Why shouldn't I like them, even if it's just a dream?

THE CLOUD Fool, you'll never be able to stop at dreaming. You will go to them. You will do something terrible. Then death will come.

IXION Tell me the names of all the goddesses.

THE CLOUD You see how you're not satisfied with just dreaming anymore? You think your dreams are real. I'm begging you, Ixion, don't go up there. Think about how the monsters were punished. They won't let you out with less.

IXION I had another dream last night. You were there too, Nephele. We were fighting the Centaurs. I had a son whose mother was a goddess—I don't know which one. I was convinced he was the same young man I saw walking in the forest. He was stronger than me, Nephele. Then the Centaurs retreated and we took the mountain. You think that's funny, Nephele? Can't you see that even in my dreams, I can accept my fate?

THE CLOUD Your fate is sealed. No one who catches the eye of a goddess goes unpunished.

IXION Not even the goddess of the oak tree, ruler of these peaks?

THE CLOUD This one, that one—it doesn't matter, Ixion. Don't be frightened though. I'll stay by your side to the end.

THE CHIMERA

Sarpedon & Hippolochus

In pursuit of glory and death, young Greek men gladly set off for the East. Their virtuous confidence led them across a sea of fantastical atrocities that not all of them could handle. It's useless to name names. For there were many more than just seven Crusades. The sadness that consumed old Bellerophon, the Chimera killer, and his grandson Sarpedon, who died at Troy, is recounted by none other than Homer in Book VI of the Iliad.

HIPPOLOCHUS Oh, there you are.

SARPEDON I saw your father. He won't even consider coming back. He's a stubborn, ugly sight, endlessly tromping around the countryside, unwashed and oblivious to the weather. Hippolochus, your father is an old bum.

HIPPOLOCHUS What do the peasants think of him?

SARPEDON The Aleion plain is desolate, Uncle. Only reeds and swamps there. I asked after him in Xanthus, but they hadn't seen him in days.

HIPPOLOCHUS And what does he say?

SARPEDON He doesn't remember us, or home. When he meets someone, he talks about the Solymi and Glaucus, and Sisyphus and the Chimera. When he saw me, he said, "Son, if I were your age, I'd have already drowned myself in the ocean." Though he wouldn't hurt a fly. "Son," he told me, "you are compassionate and just. If you want to live a just and compassionate life, you have to stop living."

HIPPOLOCHUS Was he really ranting and complaining like that?

SARPEDON He said horrible, disturbing things. He even dared the gods to compare themselves to him. He just walks, day and night. But he's not offending anyone, or mourning anyone—except for the dead and the gods.

HIPPOLOCHUS You mean Glaucus and Sisyphus?

SARPEDON He says they were treacherously punished. Why wait until they're old, sad, and beaten to ambush them? "Bellerophon," he says, "was just and compassionate when blood still coursed through his veins, but now that he is old and alone, the gods decide to abandon him?"

HIPPOLOCHUS How strange to marvel about these things. To blame the gods for something that comes for every living being . . . And what does he have in common with those dead men? He was always on the right side.

SARPEDON You know, Hippolochus, I asked myself the same thing when I saw the lost look on his face. Is this man talking, the same man who used to be

Bellerophon? Something happened to your father. It's not just that he's old. It's not just that he's sad and alone. Your father is doing penance for the Chimera.

HIPPOLOCHUS Are you out of your mind?

SARPEDON Your father blames the gods who told him to kill the Chimera for the injustice. "Since that day," he keeps saying, "when I was red with the blood of the monster, my life has never seemed real again. I sought enemies, crushed the Amazons, destroyed the Solymi, I ruled Lycia and planted a garden. . . But what does any of it mean? Where is the next Chimera? Where is the strength in these arms that killed the Chimera? Sisyphus and Glaucus, my father, were both young and noble once—then they got old and the gods betrayed them, the gods let them become animals and die. How can the man who defeated the Chimera just accept death?" That's what your father says—the man who used to be Bellerophon.

HIPPOLOCHUS Our kind pushed the limits, from Sisyphus, who chained up young Thanatos, to Glaucus, who fed his horses the flesh of living people. But these were ancient men of a gruesome time. The Chimera was the last monster seen. Now our world is just and compassionate.

SARPEDON Don't you believe, Hippolochus? Don't you think killing it should have been enough? Our father—if I can call him that—should think it was. And yet he is sad like a god, like a gray, derelict god, tromping through fields and meadows talking about dead men.

HIPPOLOCHUS But what's he missing? What?

SARPEDON He's missing his killing arm. He's missing the pride of Glaucus and Sisyphus, and he's tormented by their audacity now that, like them, he's reached his own limit, his end. He knows there will never be another Chimera waiting for him in the rocks. He's daring the gods.

HIPPOLOCHUS I am his son, Sarpedon, and I don't understand. In a compassionate world, a person should be able to grow old in peace. I understand hot bloodedness in a young man like yourself. But for a young man. For noble causes. And not for pitting yourself against the gods.

SARPEDON He knows the difference between a young man and old man. He's seen a lot. He's seen the gods the way we see each other. He tells such terrible tales.

HIPPOLOCHUS How could you listen to him?

SARPEDON Who wouldn't want to listen to him? Bellerophon has seen things no one else has.

HIPPOLOCHUS I know Sarpedon, I know, but that world is gone. He told me the same stories when I was a child.

SARPEDON Except back then he wasn't communing with the dead. They were adventure stories back then. But now, every destiny he encounters becomes his own.

HIPPOLOCHUS And then what does he say?

SARPEDON You already know some of it, but you don't know how cold his eyes have gotten, that lost look, like a man who's come to nothing but knows everything. The stories of Lydia and Phrygia, old stories, without justice or compassion. You know the one about Silenus, who was challenged to fight a god on Mount Celaenae—then the god killed him, just slaughtered him, like a butcher would a goat. Water rushes from that cave like a river of blood. Or the one about the mother who was turned to stone, into a weeping boulder, after a goddess shot deadly arrows at all her sons, one by one, just for fun. Or the story of Arachne, who was horrified by Athena's hatred and became a spider. The gods did that to her.

HIPPOLOCHUS Fine. What does it matter? It doesn't do any good to think about all that. There is nothing left of those destinies.

SARPEDON The river, the stone, the terror are still here. The dreams are still here. Bellerophon can't take a step without tripping over a corpse, or a hatred, or a puddle of blood from back when things happened, and things were not dreams. His arm had deadly clout in the world.

HIPPOLOCHUS He was a cruel man too.

SARPEDON He was just and compassionate. He killed Chimeras. Now that he is old and tired, the gods abandon him.

HIPPOLOCHUS Is that why he wanders the countryside?

SARPEDON He's the son of Sisyphus and of Glaucus. He fears fierce and capricious gods. He's starting to feel like an animal and doesn't want to die.

"My boy," he says to me, "this is the game, the ultimate betrayal: first they take all your strength and then they resent you for being less than a man. If you want to live, you have to stop living . . ."

HIPPOLOCHUS Knowing everything he knows—why doesn't he kill himself?

SARPEDON No one kills themself. Death is destiny, Hippolochus. The best you can do is hope for it.

BLIND

Oedipus & Tiresias

And yet there's no story from Thebes that doesn't include Tiresias, the blind soothsayer. The sorrows of Oedipus began shortly after this conversation—which is to say, his eyes were opened and then, in dread, he obliterated them.

OEDIPUS Old Tiresias, here in Thebes they say the gods blinded you out of jealousy. Is that what I should believe?

TIRESIAS Well, if I accepted that everything comes from them, I'd believe it too.

OEDIPUS What do you think?

TIRESIAS I think we talk too much about the gods. When it comes to bad luck, being blind isn't that different from being alive. Things go wrong when it's their time to go wrong.

OEDIPUS So what are these gods playing at?

TIRESIAS The world was here before they were. It already existed, filling space, bleeding, and delighting—it was the only god before time was born. Things themselves ruled then. Things happened. But now, it's all by virtue of the gods, and so everything is made of words, illusion, and threats. The gods make trouble—dangling things and then ripping them away. Don't touch things. Don't change things. They got here too late.

OEDIPUS Only a priest, like you, would say that?

TIRESIAS If I didn't know that much, I wouldn't be a priest. Think of a boy swimming in the Asopus. It's a summer morning. The boy climbs out of the water, happy, so he plunges back in. Again and again, he dives back into the water. Then, he hits it wrong and drowns. What do the gods have to do with that? Do we blame the gods for his death? Or thank them for his happiness? Neither. Something happened—good or bad—and it has no name, so the gods name it.

OEDIPUS Giving something a name, explaining it, does that seem so trivial to you, Tiresias?

TIRESIAS You're young, Oedipus, like the gods, and like them, you explain things by naming them. You don't know yet that there is rock under the dirt, or that the bluest sky is the emptiest. For someone like me, someone who can't see, everything is a bump, nothing more.

OEDIPUS But you've followed the gods your whole life. The changing seasons, human pleasures, human tragedy—all that has always been your concern. They tell stories about you as if you were a god. Some of the stories are so odd, so unusual, they must have meaning—like the one about the clouds in the sky.

TIRESIAS I've had quite a life. I've had such a life that every story I hear feels like my own. So, what do you think a cloudy sky means?

OEDIPUS A presence in the void . . .

TIRESIAS What is it about this story that makes you think it means something?

OEDIPUS Old Tiresias, have you always been like this?

TIRESIAS I hear you. There's the story of me and the snakes, and how I was a woman for seven years. So, what do you think that story means?

OEDIPUS You're the one it happened to, so you should know. And yet those are the sorts of things that don't happen without gods.

TIRESIAS Is that what you think? Anything can happen. Nothing is extraordinary. At the time, I was repulsed by sex—I thought that sex poisoned my spirit, my well-being, my character. When I saw those two snakes copulating and writhing on the moss, I was filled with disgust. I poked them with my stick. Then, right after that, I was a woman. For years, my pride was forced into submission. The things of this world are rock, Oedipus.

OEDIPUS But is the female sex really that vile?

TIRESIAS Not in the least. Nothing would be vile if it weren't for the gods. Sure, there are irritations, repulsions, and illusions, all of which disperse when you touch rock. In my case, the rock was the power of sex, its constancy, its omnipresence across all forms and transformations. From man to woman and then back again (seven years after seeing those two snakes). Whatever my spirit didn't want to face was forced on me or turned into lust. The arrogant man and the ravaged woman, liberated like a woman and abject like a man. In the end I knew everything about sex: as a man I sought men and as a woman I sought women.

OEDIPUS So you see, the gods did teach you something.

TIRESIAS There is no god of sex. I'm telling you, it's the rock. A lot of gods are wild animals, but the snake is the most ancient. When it flattens to the ground, it represents sex. There is life and death in the snake. What god can incarnate and comprise so much?

OEDIPUS But you—you just said—

TIRESIAS Tiresias is old and isn't a god. When he was young, he didn't pay attention. Sex is foggy and always equivocal. It's a half that feels like a whole. Man embodies it, inhabiting it like a strong swimmer in the water—but in the meantime, he's aged, he's touched the rock. At the end there's this idea, this lingering illusion, that the other sex has been satisfied. Well, don't believe it. I know it's futile for everyone.

OEDIPUS It's not easy to argue with what you say. It's not for nothing your story begins with snakes. But it also begins with disgust and the nuisance of sex. And what would you tell a real man who swears he's not disgusted?

TIRESIAS That he's not a real man—he's still a child.

OEDIPUS But I too have had encounters on the road to Thebes. One time I was talking about man—his journey from birth to death—and we touched the rock too. After that, I became a husband, and father, and king of Thebes. There's nothing ambiguous or futile about my life.

TIRESIAS You're not the only one, Oedipus, who thinks that. But the rock isn't touched by words. May the gods protect you. I can talk to you too, but I am old. Only the blind know darkness. I feel like I live outside of time and have always been alive, and I no longer believe in days. There's also something in me that feels pleasure and bleeds.

OEDIPUS You said this something was a god. Why won't you try praying to him, dear Tiresias?

TIRESIAS Everyone prays to some kind of god, but what happens is unnamable. What does the boy drowning on a summer morning know of the gods? What's the use of praying? There is a big snake for every day of life, flattening to the ground and watching. Did you ever wonder, Oedipus, why the unhappy ones go blind as they age?

OEDIPUS I pray to the gods that doesn't happen to me.

FILLIES

Hermes chthonius & the Centaur Chiron

There's no need to say more about Hermes, that liminal god, straddling life and death, sex and spirit, between the mortal Titans and the gods of Olympus. Whereas the good doctor Asclepius, emerging from a divine world of animal metamorphoses—he's worth saying something about.

HERMES The God wants you to raise this child, son of beautiful Coronis. You already know she died. And how the God reached his immortal hands into the flames and ripped the baby from her womb. I'd been summoned to her tragic, still-burning corpse, hair blazing like a field of straw. But her shadow didn't even wait for me. It leaped off the pyre and disappeared into Hades.

CHIRON Did she come back from that crossing as a filly?

HERMES That's what I think. Her mane and those flames were so similar. But I didn't have time to make sure. I had to grab the baby and bring him up here.

CHIRON Little baby, you would have been better off just staying in the fire. You got nothing from your mother except her sad, human form. You are the son of a cruel and blinding light, and you will occupy a world of bloodless, suffering shadows, of infected flesh, of fever and endless sighs. You're just like your father, the Radiant One. The light that made you scours the world implacable, illuminating sadness, decrepitude, and the pitifulness of it all. May the serpents watch over you.

HERMES Yesterday's world must really be extinct if even the serpents have passed into the Radiance. But can't you tell me why she had to die?

HERMES We will never again watch her bounding from the peak of Didymus to the peak of Mount Pelion, through reeds and over the cliffs. Yet this is all we have. Words are blood.

HERMES Believe me when I tell you, Chiron, I miss her as much as the rest of you. But I swear I don't know why the God killed her. In my hometown of Larissa, I hear talk of bestiality, meetings in grottos and the woods . . .

CHIRON What does that mean? We're all beasts. Even you, spawned by a bull in Larissa—and at the beginning of time, you were mixed in swamp mud with all the unformed flesh and blood there was in the world—and yet, you're shocked?

HERMES That was a long time ago, Chiron, and now I live underground and at thresholds. Sometimes I watch you all, storming down the mountain like boulders, jumping puddles and gorges, chasing each other, calling out, romping. I know you have hoofs and your nature, but that's not all you are. Your manly arms and chest, for instance, and that great human laugh, and the murdered woman, making love with God, and the friends who now weep for her—are all different. Why, even your mother, if I'm not mistaken, caught the eye of a god.

CHIRON That was indeed another time. The old god turned himself into a stallion to woo her. On the mountain peak.

HERMES Then tell me why beautiful Coronis, who strolled through vineyards and dallied with the Radiant One, was killed and her body burned?

CHIRON How often have you been able to see Mount Olympus from Larissa, the way it stands out against the sky after a windy night?

HERMES I can not only see it, but I go up there.

CHIRON There was a time when we galloped up there too, racing from ridge to ridge.

HERMES You should go back.

CHIRON My friend . . . Coronis went back.

HERMES What do you mean by that?

CHIRON What I mean is that it's death. That's where the rulers are. Not rulers like Kronos the elder, or his ancient father, or even us—back in the days that we might have thought such things, back when our joy had no boundaries, leaping here and there, being ourselves. That was when the beasts and the marsh were where men and gods met. The mountain the horse the grass the dew the waterfall—we were everything under the sun. Who could die back then? What did bestial mean if the beast was in us, as the gods were in us?

HERMES You have daughters, Chiron. They are women and fillies by choice. What are you complaining about? You have the mountains and the plains, the changing seasons. You don't even lack, for the pleasure it gives you, human settlements, homes and villages on the edges of the valley, the barns and the hearths, where melancholy mortals make up stories about you and always welcome you. Don't you think the world is better off under these new rulers?

CHIRON You are one of them and you defend them. You were once all fury and drive, now you lead bloodless shadows underground. What are these mortals if not shadows before their time? And yet I take pleasure in the notion that this baby's mother leaped before you, all by herself. If nothing else, she found herself in death.

HERMES Now I know why she died. The woman who climbed the mountain, who loved a god completely, so much that she birthed this child. You say the God was merciless, but couldn't you also say that she left animal lust behind her in the marsh, that shapeless bloody fury that created her?

CHIRON Certainly not. But does it matter?

HERMES The new gods of Thessalia laugh a lot. The only thing they can't laugh about is chaos—believe me, I've seen destiny. Whenever chaos overwhelms the light, their light, they have to reconstitute, destroy and rebuild. That is why Coronis had to die.

CHIRON But they can't rebuild Coronis. I was right when I said that Olympus is death.

HERMES And yet, the Radiant One loved her. He would have grieved for her too if he wasn't a god. He tore the baby from her body. It is with joy he entrusts his baby to you. He knows that you are the only one who can make a real man of him.

CHIRON I already told you the fate that awaits such mortals. The baby will be Asclepius, the god of human bodies, a man-god. He will live amid infected flesh and much sighing. Men will come to him to escape fate, to put off the agony for one more night, for one moment. This child will move between life and death like you, once bull semen and now nothing more than a guide for shadows. This is the fate the Olympians will levy on those living on earth.

HERMES Isn't it better for mortals to end up this way, rather than how ancient damnation would have them: transformed into flora and fauna, made into cows that low, serpents that snake, eternal rocks or weeping springs?

CHIRON As long as Olympus rules the sky, sure, yes. But this too will pass.

THE FLOWER

Eros & Thanatos

It is so glaringly evident that we won't be shocked by Apollo the Radiant, nubile god, despite these accounts of such atrocious tenderness, given by those Leopardians, Eros and Thanatos.

EROS Were you expecting something like this to happen?

THANATOS I expect anything from an Olympian. But I didn't expect it to turn out this way, no.

EROS Thankfully, the mortals will call it an accident.

THANATOS It isn't the first time, nor will it be the last.

EROS And in the meantime Hyacinthus is dead. His sisters are in mourning. The useless flower born from his spilled blood, now blankets the Eurotas River. Spring has come, Thanatos, but the boy won't see it.

THANATOS These flowers bloom wherever an immortal passes. But there was at least a pretext all the other times, a flight, some offense. Someone attacking a god or inflicting an impropriety. Think of what happened to Daphne, to Linus, to Actaeon. Yet Hyacinthus was just a boy. He spent his days venerating the god. He played with him as children play. He was stunned and transfixed. You know, Eros, you know.

EROS The mortals are already speaking of it as an accident. No one's considered that the Radiant One doesn't tend to miss his mark.

THANATOS All I could see was that twisted smile following the flight of the discus, then watching it fall. The discus went high, toward the sun, and Hyacinthus lifted his hand to shield his eyes and it struck him on the forehead. Why did that happen, Eros? Surely you know.

EROS What can I tell you, Thanatos? I can't let myself go soft over some whim. You know as well as I do that whenever a god gets close to a mortal, something cruel comes of it. You yourself have told the story of Daphne and Actaeon.

THANATOS So what was it this time?

EROS I told you, a whim. The Radiant One wanted to play. He descended among mortals and saw Hyacinthus. They were together for six days in Amyclae, six days that changed Hyacinthus's heart and revitalized the soil. But when the god was ready to leave, Hyacinthus showed disappointment. Then the discus landed between his eyes . . .

THANATOS Who knows . . . perhaps the Radiant One didn't want him to cry.

EROS The Radiant One knows nothing about tears. We're the ones who know, young gods and demons, those of us who were alive back when Olympus was just a bare mountain. We've seen so much, we've even seen the trees and rocks weep. This god is different. Six days or a lifetime, it's all the same to him. No one knows that more fully than Hyacinthus.

THANATOS You don't really think Hyacinthus understood such things? That the god had been something more to him than an idol, an older friend, a trusted and beloved brother? I saw his face when his hands were lifted, there was nothing there but trust and surprise. Hyacinthus had no idea he was playing with the Radiant One.

EROS Anything is possible, Thanatos. It could also be that the boy didn't know about Linus and Daphne. It's so difficult to say where discomfort ends and trust begins. No doubt he had six full days of restless passion.

THANATOS What do you think was in his heart?

EROS What's in the heart of every young man. But this time, the object of his thoughts and actions was too much for a boy. He talked to his guest in the gymnasium, in the hallways, as they walked together along the banks of the Eurotas, talking and listening. He heard the stories of Delos and Delphi, Typho, Thessaly, and the land of the Hyperboreans. The god wore a serene smile as he spoke, like a traveler who everyone thought was dead but who came back wiser. I'm certain the god never spoke of Olympus, his immortal companions, or divine matters. He talked about himself, his sisters, the muses the way anyone would talk about their family—wonderful and intimate. Sometimes they would listen to a wandering poet invited in for the night.

THANATOS There's nothing amiss in any of that.

EROS Nothing amiss . . . it was even reassuring. Hyacinthus learned that the god from Delos, with his indescribable eyes and soothing voice, had seen and experienced worldly things that might also happen to him one day. The visitor talked about Hyacinthus too, his people, his humble life in Amyclae, all of it bright and familiar. They did things together. He treated Hyacinthus like an equal, a peer, and spoke the names of the forbidding, smiling young women—Aglaia, Euphrosyne, and Thalia—saying how they lived with him in a mysteriously intimate way. He was so carefree when he spoke of them, and had such an appetite for leisure, it made Hyacinthus's heart tremble. This is what he did to the boy. With the god, everything was easy and bright. To Hyacinthus then anything seemed possible.

THANATOS I've known other mortals. Those more expert, wiser, stronger than Hyacinthus. All destroyed by this mania to do everything.

EROS Oh, my dear, all Hyacinthus really had was hope, an apprehensive hope he might eventually be like his guest. The Radiant One couldn't see it, didn't pick up on the enthusiasm in the boy's eyes—it was enough to evoke hope. Instead, he saw in his eyes and curly locks the lovely, mottled blossoms that would be Hyacinthus's fate. He thought nothing of words, or tears. He'd come to see a flower. This flower had to be worthy of him—marvelous and cozy, like his memory of the Graces. He created this flower from his indolence.

THANATOS We are so ferocious, we immortals. I ask myself how much longer the Olympians will set destiny. All that daring, but it's possibly what will destroy them.

EROS Who can say? From the time of chaos, there's been nothing but blood. Blood of men, monsters, and gods. One begins in blood and dies in blood. How do you think you were born?

THANATOS Being born means having to die. Even men know that. But the Olympians don't. They've forgotten. They endure while the world passes. They don't exist; they are. Every one of their whims is a death sentence. They have to destroy someone in order to express a flower.

EROS Yes, Thanatos. But shouldn't we consider the richness of the ideas that were put to Hyacinthus? That nervous hope that was his death was also birth. He was a young man, unaware, a little wayward, still drowsy from childhood, son of Amyclas, modest lord of a modest land. What would he have been without the visitor from Delos?

THANATOS A man among men, Eros.

EROS I know. And I also know that there is no escape from fate. But I'm not used to caring about such folly. Hyacinthus lived six days in the shadow of this light. He didn't miss out on perfect joy or on a fast, bitter end. Those are things the immortals and the Olympians can't know. What more would you want for him, Thanatos?

THANATOS I'd want the Radiant One to mourn him as we do.

EROS You ask too much.

BEAST

Endymion & a stranger

We believe Artemis's love for Endymion wasn't carnal. And yet that doesn't exclude the very real possibility that the feebler of the two lusted for blood. The virgin goddess is known for her unwholesome character—she who ruled the beasts and came into the world from the forbidden dark forest of divine mothers of the monstrous Mediterranean. Just as it is known that a person who can't sleep wants to sleep and goes down in history as the eternal dreamer.

ENDYMION You—walking by—can we talk? I can talk to you because you're not from around here. Don't worry about the madness in my eyes, the rags on your feet are as disreputable. But you seem like a serious man who will eventually settle down in some nice village, where you will relax, find work and a home—because that's what you want. And yet I'm pretty sure you wander now because all you have is fate. You walk these roads at dawn, which must mean that you like to be awake when things are just emerging from the night, still untouched. You see Mount Latmus over there? I go up there all the time at night, when it's darkest, and wait among the beech trees for dawn. And yet I feel like I've never stepped foot there.

STRANGER Who can claim he's stepped everywhere he's been, anyway?

ENDYMION I think sometimes we're impalpable, like the rushing wind. Or like the dreams of a sleeping person. Do you like to sleep during the day, stranger?

STRANGER Well, whenever. If I'm tired, I sleep.

ENDYMION And when you sleep, wanderer, do you ever listen to the wind blowing, or the birds, or swamps, the bustle, the water's voice? Have you ever felt that when you're sleeping, you're never alone?

STRANGER I wouldn't know, friend. I've always been on my own.

ENDYMION I get no peace from sleep, stranger. I always think I've been sleeping but I know it's not true.

STRANGER You seem in good shape to me—and strong.

ENDYMION I am, I am. And I know the sleep of wine, and that deep sleep at a woman's side. But none of that does me any good. Now, when I go to sleep, my ears are always perked, and my eyes—I have these eyes, like a man who stares into the darkness. I feel like I've always been this way.

STRANGER Have you lost someone?

ENDYMION Someone? Oh stranger, do you really think we're mortal?

STRANGER Someone died on you?

ENDYMION Not someone . . . When I go up Mount Latmus, I stop being mortal. Don't look at my eyes, they don't count. I know I'm not dreaming—it's been so long since I've slept. You see that clump of trees, up on the cliff? That's where I was last night, waiting for her.

STRANGER Who were you waiting for?

ENDYMION Let's not name her. We will not say her name. She has no name. Or maybe she has too many. My friend, do you know how terrifying the forest is when a nocturnal glen opens up? No? Imagine the nocturnal glen, some place you passed through during the day—there's a pretty flower, some berry bushes over there rustling in the breeze, more berries, this flower—it's a wild, untouchable, mortal thing among wild things. Get it? A flower that's like a wild animal? My friend, have you ever felt both fear of and desire for the essence of a she-wolf, or a doe, or a snake?

STRANGER You mean, lust for a wild animal?

ENDYMION Yes, but not just that. Have you ever known someone who was many things at once, who contains all—every gesture, every thought you've had about her—she holds vast things from your world, your sky, and your words, memories, days past you'll never know, future days, everything you're sure of, and another world, another sky that you can't have?

STRANGER I've heard talk of such things.

ENDYMION And, what if this person were the beast, the wild thing, the untouchable nature that has no name?

STRANGER What dreadful things you're saying.

ENDYMION But that's not all. You should listen to me. When you set back out on the road, you should know the earth is full of divinity and horror. If I tell you all this it's because you and I, as travelers and strangers, we have a little divinity of our own, too.

STRANGER Of course I have seen many things. And some of them dreadful. But you don't need to cross great distances. If it helps, I can tell you that immortals also feel the lure of the hearth.

ENDYMION So you do know, and you believe me! I was napping one night on Latmus—it was dark—I had been out late walking, and I fell asleep sitting against a tree trunk. When I woke the moon was high—but in my dream I shivered slightly at the notion that I was there in the glen and then I saw her. She was watching me, with those slightly unfocused but steady eyes—transparent and vast. I didn't know it then, or even the next day, but I already belonged to her. I'd come into her sights, the space she occupies, the glen, the mountain. She barely smiled at me, and I said, "My lady," which made her frown like a feral girl, like she'd figured out that I was in her thrall, and I was a little dismayed to have called her a lady. Then an uneasiness hung between us.

She said my name, stranger, and came closer—her tunic was short, above her knees—she reached out and touched my hair. She was almost hesitant, and then she really smiled. It was an incredible smile. It seemed mortal. I was about to bow down, rehearsing all her different names, but she stopped me, the way you stop a child, put her hand under my chin. You can see that I'm a big, strong man, but she was proud and had those eyes—she was just a thin, wild girl—and I was like a little boy. "You must never wake up," she told me.

"You don't have to do a thing. I will come find you." Then she crossed the glen and disappeared.

That whole night I walked Mount Latmus. I followed the moon into every stream, into crevices, up to the peaks. My ears were alert but full, like with the ocean, full of that cold, raspy, motherly voice. I stopped at every rustling or shadow. I could only see the flight of wild animals. When dawn came, with its bruised, veiled light, I looked down at this plain—at this road we're walking together now, and I knew that I would never again live among men. I was no longer one of them. I would wait for nightfall.

STRANGER What remarkable stories you tell, Endymion. And what's really remarkable is that you undoubtedly went back up the mountain, and you walk there and live there now and yet this wild creature, the woman with many names, still hasn't made you hers.

ENDYMION Stranger, I am hers.

STRANGER I meant to say . . . Haven't you heard the story about her and the shepherd, who was ripped apart by dogs for his indiscretion . . . the man-stag?

ENDYMION I know everything about her, stranger. Because we have talked and talked while I pretend to sleep. It's like that every night, and I haven't touched her, the way you wouldn't touch a lioness or the green water in a pond, or that which is more yours than anything and holds your heart. Listen. She stands before me—this thin, unsmiling girl—and she watches me. Her vast, transparent eyes have seen so much. Still see. Possessing with those eyes. There's a berry in her eyes and there's the beast, there is screaming and death, the cruel entreaty.

I know this bloodshed, this torn flesh, the ravenous earth, the solitude. For her, savage goddess, this is solitude. For her, the beast is solitude. She touches me the way one would pet a dog or feel the trunk of a tree. But she watches me. This thin girl in a short tunic, so much like any girl you'd see in your own village.

STRANGER Endymion, haven't you told her anything about your life as a man?

ENDYMION Stranger, you know such dreadful things and yet you don't know that the savage and the divine cancel out the man?

STRANGER I know that when you go up Latmus you stop being mortal. But immortals know how to be alone. And you dislike solitude. You look for sex in beasts. You pretend to sleep when she's there. What exactly have you asked of her?

ENDYMION If she would only smile again. I would bleed for her, be the flesh in her dog's mouth.

STRANGER And how does she answer?

ENDYMION She says nothing. She watches me. She leaves me alone at dawn. And I search for her among the trees. The daylight hurts my eyes. "You should never wake up," she tells me.

STRANGER Mortal man, the day you are truly awake is the day you will know why she's protected you from her smile.

ENDYMION I already know, stranger, Stranger who talks like a god.

STRANGER The earth is crowned by both the divine and the awful, and we walk these roads. You've been saying that very thing.

ENDYMION Oh itinerate god, her tenderness is like dawn, it is the earth and sky revealed. It is divinity. But toward the others, the things and beasts—the savage has a brusque laugh and a vicious rule. No one has ever touched her knee.

STRANGER Endymion, let your mortal heart settle. Neither god nor man has touched it. Her raspy, motherly voice is everything and all that savage can ever give you.

ENDYMION And yet.

STRANGER And yet?

ENDYMION As long as the mountain is there, I will not sleep in peace.

STRANGER Everyone has their own kind of sleep, Endymion. Your sleep is a plethora of voices, cries, of earth, sky, days. Sleep with courage, you have nothing else worthwhile. Savage solitude is yours. Love her like she loves. And now, Endymion, I must leave you. You will see her tonight.

ENDYMION Thank you, itinerant god.

STRANGER Farewell. And remember, you must never again wake up.

SEA FOAM

Sappho & Britomartis

Callimachus tells the story of Britomartis, a nymph of Cretan and Minoan descent. Sappho was a lesbian from Lesbos, unfortunate fact, but sadder still was her disappointment in life—the reason why she threw herself into the sea. The Greek Sea is full of islands, with Cyprus, where Aphrodite was born from the foam, at the easternmost point. This sea bore witness to great passions and such misfortune. Do I even need to invoke the names? Ariadne, Phaedra, Andromache, Elle, Scilla, Io, Cassandra, Medea. All of them went into this same sea, and more than one of them stayed. It gives the idea that all the water is soaked with sperm and tears.

SAPPHO It's monotonous here, Britomartis. The sea is monotonous. You've been here ages. Don't you ever get bored?

BRITOMARTIS I know you liked being mortal better. Being the foam on a wave isn't enough for you. And yet you were seeking death, this death. Why?

SAPPHO I didn't know it would be like this. I thought everything would end when I jumped. I thought my desire and restlessness and all my turmoil would disappear. The sea swallows. The sea annihilates. That's what I told myself.

BRITOMARTIS Everything dies in the sea and is reborn. Now you know.

SAPPHO You were a nymph, Britomartis. What were you trying to find in the sea?

BRITOMARTIS I wasn't looking for the sea. I lived in the mountains. I fled by moonlight, chased by a mortal, I don't even know who. But then you aren't familiar with our mountains and forests, or the cliffs that loom over the sea. I jumped to save myself, Sappho.

SAPPHO To save yourself? But how?

BRITOMARTIS To escape him. To be myself. Because I had to, Sappho.

SAPPHO Did you have to? Did you hate this mortal so much?

BRITOMARTIS I don't know. I didn't see him. I only knew that I had to escape.

SAPPHO That seems unbelievable. You leave days behind, the mountains and fields—you leave solid ground to become sea foam—because you had to? You had to . . . What? Didn't you want anything? Weren't you full of longing, like me?

BRITOMARTIS I don't understand you, lovely Sappho. Longing and restlessness made you who you are; so why can't you understand why I'd want escape, too?

SAPPHO You were never mortal. You knew there was no escape.

BRITOMARTIS I didn't escape longing, Sappho. I have everything I desire. I once was a mountain nymph, now I am a sea nymph. That's how we're made. Our life is leaves and trees, spurting water, and seafoam. We play at making things bloom, not escaping. We don't escape. We change. That's our fate and our desire. Our only terror is that of being possessed, trapped by a man. That would be the end. Do you know Calypso's story?

SAPPHO I've heard of her.

BRITOMARTIS Calypso let herself be caught by a man. Then everything stopped mattering to her. She wouldn't leave her cave for years and years. They all came—Leucothea, Calianira, Cymodoce, Orithyia, even Amphitrite—they tried talking to her, getting her to leave with them. At last they saved her but it took years, and it wasn't until after that man left.

SAPPHO I understand Calypso. But I don't understand why she listened to you all. What's desire if you can just give it up like that?

BRITOMARTIS Oh deadly wave, won't you ever know what it's like to smile?

SAPPHO I knew when I was alive. And I sought death.

BRITOMARTIS That is not smiling, Sappho. To smile is to live like an ocean wave or the leaf on a tree, to accept fate. To die in one form and be born another. It is to accept, accept oneself and destiny.

SAPPHO So you've accepted it?

BRITOMARTIS I fled, Sappho. It is easier for us.

SAPPHO Back when I knew all about escape, too. My kind of escape was making a song, or words, out of the turmoil, out of anything. But destiny is another matter.

BRITOMARTIS Why? Destiny is joy, and when you sang, the song was happy.

SAPPHO I was never happy. Desire is not a song, Britomartis. Desire beats and burns like the serpent, like the wind.

BRITOMARTIS Didn't you know any mortal women at peace with their own desire and turmoil?

SAPPHO Not one . . . maybe, yes one . . . But not a mortal like Sappho was. When you were still a mountain nymph before I was born, there was a woman who crossed this very sea, a mortal whose life was constant turmoil. Maybe she was at peace with it. This woman killed, destroyed, and blinded like a goddess—she was always true to herself. Maybe she didn't even have to smile. She was beautiful, not foolish, and everyone around her fought and died. They fought and died—wanting only for a moment to join her name with their own. That she would give her name to their lives and their deaths. They smiled for her. You know her . . . Helen of Troy, daughter of Leda.

BRITOMARTIS And she was happy?

SAPPHO She didn't run away, that much is certain. She was happy with herself. She didn't question her destiny. And anyone strong enough, willful enough, could take her. For ten years she was with a hero; they took her away from him and married her to someone else, and then he lost her too, and as there were many men across the sea fighting on her behalf, the second one took her back; she lived happily with him; she was buried; and when she got to Hades, she met more men. She never lied to anyone; she never smiled at anyone. Maybe she was happy.

BRITOMARTIS And you envy this person?

SAPPHO I don't envy anyone. I wanted to die. Just becoming a different person wouldn't have been enough for me. If I can't be Sappho, I'd rather be nothing.

BRITOMARTIS So you accept destiny?

SAPPHO I don't accept it. I am it. No one accepts it.

BRITOMARTIS Except for those of us who know how to smile.

SAPPHO What splendid power. It's your destiny. But what does it mean?

BRITOMARTIS It means to accept the self and accept others.

SAPPHO What does that mean? How do you accept some force that overwhelms you, making you into desire, a quivering desire twisted around a body—someone, a man or woman—like foam on the reef? But this body resists you, ruins you, and you fall again, you want to hug the rocky shore, you want to accept it. Then, there are the times when you are the shore and the foam—the turmoil. It all swirls around your feet. No one is ever peaceful. How can you accept all of that?

BRITOMARTIS You must accept it. You wanted to escape and now you're foam too.

SAPPHO But don't you feel this tedium, this restless tide? Everything constantly soaking and simmering. Even what's dead flounders restlessly.

BRITOMARTIS You're from an island yourself, you should know about the sea . . .

SAPPHO I've been terrified of it ever since I was little. This endless life is monotonous and sad, Britomartis. There are no words to describe the tedium.

BRITOMARTIS Once, back on my island, I watched the mortals come and go. There were women like you, Sappho, women of love. They didn't seem sad or weary to me.

SAPPHO I know, I know. But did you follow them after they left? One of them hanged herself on the crossbeams of her house in a foreign land. Another woke one morning to find herself on an abandoned beach. And the others, so many others, from the islands, from everywhere, coming to the water—some enslaved, others tortured, another killed her own children, another struggled day and night, and then there was the woman who never again stepped on dry land and became something else, a sea monster.

BRITOMARTIS But Helen, you said, came out unscathed.

SAPPHO Sowing massacre and fire. She didn't smile at anyone. She didn't lie to anyone. She was worthy of the sea. Remember who was born here, Britomartis . . .

BRITOMARTIS Who do you mean?

SAPPHO There's an island you haven't seen yet. It's the first one hit by sunlight at dawn . . .

BRITOMARTIS Oh, Sappho.

SAPPHO . . . She emerges from the foam, the one with no name, tormented, restless, smiling to herself.

BRITOMARTIS But she's not suffering. She's a great goddess.

SAPPHO And everything that soaks and flounders in the sea is her matter and her breath. Have you seen her?

BRITOMARTIS Don't ask me, Sappho. I'm only a little nymph.

SAPPHO So you have . . .

BRITOMARTIS We all run from her, child. Let's not speak of her.

THE MOTHER

Meleager & Hermes

Meleager's life was bound to a burning ember his mother, Althaea, pulled from the fire when he was born. An imperious mother, who, consumed by rage after Meleager killed his uncle—her brother—in a dispute over who deserved the hide of the slain boar, hurled the ember back into the flames, leaving it there to burn.

MELEAGER I was burned like kindling, Hermes.

HERMES But you must not have suffered much.

MELEAGER The pain, the passion of before, was worse.

HERMES And now, Meleager, you're dead. The flames, all that burning—it's all in the past. Even the smoke that rises from the fire is more than you are. You're essentially nothing. So, accept it. All those worldly things—the places, morning, evening—none of it means anything to you now. Look around you.

MELEAGER I don't see a thing and it doesn't matter. I am still smoldering . . . What are you saying about the places of the world? Oh Hermes, you're a god, with a god's eyes, and for you the world is beautiful, odd, tender. That's what you see, Hermes. But I, Meleager, I'm just a hunter, son of hunters. I never left the woods I grew up in, I was tied to the hearth and my fate was sealed from the moment I was born from the burning ember my mother pulled from the fire. I didn't know anyone except for a few friends, the animals, and my mother.

HERMES Do you think that man, any man, has ever had more than that?

MELEAGER I couldn't say. I've heard stories of men leading carefree lives on the other side of the mountain, across the rivers, of journeys, archipelagos, encounters with monsters and gods—stories of men who are stronger than me, younger than me, men marked by strange destinies.

HERMES They all had mothers, Meleager. And they had tasks to complete. Death awaited them because of someone's love. No one is master of themselves, nor can anyone know another person.

MELEAGER A mother . . . none like mine. No one ever understood what it felt like to know she held my life in her hands, and to burn, see her looking into the fire. All because the day I was born, she extracted that ember and kept it from burning? I had to grow up and become Meleager, cry, play, hunt, see winter, watch the seasons change, be a person—yet also know this other thing, carry the weight of it in my heart, contend every day with my fate. This is punishment. Enemies don't compare.

HERMES You mortals are strange creatures. You're amazed by what you know. Obviously having an enemy isn't a big deal. Nor is having a mother. Why is it so unbearable to know your life is in her hands?

MELEAGER Hunters like us, Hermes, we have a pact. When we scale a mountain we spot each other—we hold each other's lives in our hands, but we don't betray a partner.

HERMES You fool, you only ever betray your partner . . . But that's not this. Your life is always embers, and your mother pulled you from the flames, and so you live half in ash. It's always a mother's love that gets you in the end. For, what are you if not her flesh and blood?

MELEAGER You had to have seen her eyes, Hermes. You had to have seen them from when you were little to know them so well and feel them watching your every move, every step, every day, every year, and to know they grow old, they die, they suffer, they feel that pain, and you are terrified of offending them. So yes, it is unacceptable that they stare into the fire and watch the embers.

HERMES You know all this and yet you're surprised. The fact that her eyes grow old and will die, means that in the meantime you've become a man and if you offend, you go look for something more alive and more true. But if you find those eyes—and you'll always find them, Meleager—whoever has those eyes is still your mother. You'll lose track of who you're dealing with, and you'll almost feel happy, but keep in mind that they know—old woman, young woman, they all know. No one born from fire can escape destiny.

MELEAGER There are other people who share my destiny?

HERMES They all do, Meleager, everyone. Everyone awaits a death that comes from someone's love. The mother roars through the flesh and blood of every person. And most are cowards—far more so than you.

MELEAGER I was not a coward, Hermes.

HERMES I'm talking to you as a shadow, not a mortal. So long as man doesn't know, he's brave.

MELEAGER It is not cowardly for me look around. I know so much now. But I don't believe that she, the young woman, had seen those eyes.

HERMES She didn't see them—she was them.

MELEAGER Oh Atalanta, I wonder if you will be a mother too, and capable of looking into the fire.

HERMES Try to remember what she said the night you defeated the boar.

MELEAGER That night. The night of the pact. I won't forget it. Atalanta was furious because I'd let the boar escape into the snow. She hurled her axe at me and struck my shoulder. I barely felt the blow, but I got angrier and yelled, "Go home. Go back to the women. This is no place for a silly girl." That evening, after the boar was killed, Atalanta walked at my side along with our group and she handed me the axe that she'd gone back alone to find in the snow. That was when we made a pact that whenever we went hunting, one of us would go unarmed so the other wouldn't be tempted to violence.

HERMES And what did Atalanta say to you?

MELEAGER I haven't forgotten, Hermes. "Son of Althea," she said, "we'll spread the boar skin on our bed the night of our wedding. It will be the price of your blood . . . and mine." Then she smiled, as if asking forgiveness.

HERMES No mortal man, Meleager, can think of his mother as a girl. But doesn't it strike you that a woman who says such things is also capable of looking into the fire? Old Althea killed you for the price of blood.

MELEAGER This is all my destiny, Hermes. But haven't there been mortals who lived happily without their lives in someone's hands . . .

HERMES Don't you know, Meleager? They would be gods. Sure, some coward managed to hide his head, but he still had the blood of his mother in his veins, and the hatred and passion, too, all that fury that stoked his heart. There were nights in his life where he felt that burning. You died of it, that's true, and not everyone does. Once you know, every one of you goes on to lead your lives as if dead. Believe me, Meleager, you were one of the lucky ones.

MELEAGER But to never meet my children . . . I barely knew my own bed . . .

HERMES You are fortunate. Your children won't be born. Your bed is deserted. Your companions will go hunting just the same without you. You are a shadow and are nothing.

MELEAGER But, Atalanta?

HERMES The house stands empty as if it were night and you were late returning from the hunt. Atalanta, the one who drove you to exact revenge, didn't die. The two women live together but never speak. They stare at the fireplace where your mother's brother was cut down and where you were turned to ash. Maybe they don't even hate each other. They know each other too well. Without men, the women are nothing.

MELEAGER Then why did they kill us?

HERMES Ask why they made you, Meleager.

THESE TWO

Achilles & Patroclus

There's no need to redo Homer. What we're really interested in is the conversation that took place on the night before Patroclus died.

ACHILLES Patroclus, why do men always try to boost their courage by saying, "I've seen worse." Instead, we should say, "The worst is yet to come. We'll all be corpses one day."

PATROCLUS It's like I don't know you anymore.

ACHILLES But I know you. It takes more than a little wine to kill Patroclus. I'm thinking tonight that, everything considered, there's no difference between us and the cowards. Everyone has something worse ahead. And the worst comes last. It comes after everything else and fills your mouth like a fistful of dirt. I find it reassuring to remember, "I've seen this . . . and I've suffered that . . ." But doesn't it seem unfair that we won't remember the worst thing that will ever happen to us?

PATROCLUS At least one of us will be able to remember it for the other. That's something to hope for. That's how we cheat fate.

ACHILLES And that's why we drink. Haven't you ever thought that children don't drink because death doesn't exist for them yet? Did you drink when you were young, Patroclus?

PATROCLUS I've never done anything that wasn't just what you were doing, and never anything without you.

ACHILLES I mean, back when we were always together, playing and hunting, when the days seemed short and the years were endless, did you think about death, your death? Because boys kill, but don't understand death. Then that day comes when, all of a sudden, you understand death is a part of you and that's when you become a man. Then you fight and play, drink, and get restless at night. But have you ever seen a drunk child?

PATROCLUS I wonder when the first time was. I don't know. I can't remember. Can't remember a time when I didn't drink and ignore death.

ACHILLES You're like a child, Patroclus.

PATROCLUS Ask what your enemies think of that, Achilles.

ACHILLES I will. So, death doesn't exist for you. But it's the fear of death that makes a good soldier, right?

PATROCLUS And yet tonight we drink together.

ACHILLES But don't you have memories Patroclus? Don't you ever say, "I've done this. I've seen this"? Don't you ask yourself what you've actually accomplished, or what your life's been about, what you're going to leave behind on earth or in the sea? What's the point of getting through each day if you can't remember it?

PATROCLUS When we were boys together, Achilles, we didn't remember anything. We were happy enough just to spend all our time together.

ACHILLES I wonder if there is anyone left in Thessaly who remembers how it was back then. And when our comrades over there return from this war, some will walk those roads. Will they know that we also walked there when we were boys—just as there are probably other boys there now. Do those boys know what will become of them when they grow up?

PATROCLUS That's not how children think.

ACHILLES There are days to come that we'll never see.

PATROCLUS Haven't we already seen a lot of days?

ACHILLES Not that many, Patroclus, no. One day we'll be corpses. Our mouths will be stuffed with fistfuls of dirt. Then we won't know what we've been through.

PATROCLUS There's no use thinking about that.

ACHILLES It's impossible not to. When you're a child you think you're going to live forever. You watch everything and you laugh. You don't know the cost. You don't know exhaustion and regret. Fighting is for play; you fall down dead, then you laugh and go back to the game.

PATROCLUS We've had other games. Bed and booty. The enemy. And drinking here tonight . . . Achilles, when are we heading back out onto the battlefield?

ACHILLES We're going back, you can be sure of that. Fate awaits us. When those ships go up in flames, you'll know it's time.

PATROCLUS But now?

ACHILLES Why? Are you scared? Haven't you already seen worse?

PATROCLUS It's making me crazy. We're here to finish this. Maybe tomorrow.

ACHILLES Don't be in such a rush, Patroclus. Let the gods work out *tomorrow*. Only they know what has been and will be.

PATROCLUS But seeing worse depends on us. Drink, Achilles. To the bitter end! To the sword and the shield. That which has been, will be again. We return to danger.

ACHILLES I drink to the mortals and to the immortals, Patroclus. To my father and mother. To the memory of what has been. And to the two of us.

PATROCLUS You have so many memories?

ACHILLES No more than a working girl or a beggar. They were young once too.

PATROCLUS You are fortunate, Achilles, but that fortune might as well be a rag to be thrown away. Only you would compare yourself to a beggar. You fought and conquered the Tenedos range, you split the Amazonian belt, you faced bears up on the mountain. Who else's mother tempered them in fire when they were a baby? You, Achilles, are the sword and the spear.

ACHILLES You have always been at my side, except for when I was in bathed in fire.

PATROCLUS The way a shadow follows the cloud. Like Theseus with Pirithous. Maybe one day, Achilles, you will come to Hades to rescue me. Then we'll have lived through that too.

ACHILLES It was better back before there was Hades. We played in the forests and streams and wiped off our sweat. We were just kids. Back then, every move we made, every gesture, was part of a game. We were memory but didn't know it. Were we brave? Who knows? It doesn't matter. I know it was summer on the mountain of the Centaur, then winter, then all of life. We were immortal.

PATROCLUS But something worse came along. Danger and death arrived. Then we were soldiers.

ACHILLES You can't escape fate. I didn't get to see my son. Deidamia is dead too. Why didn't I just stay on the island with the women?

PATROCLUS You wouldn't have much to remember then, Achilles. You'd still be just a kid. It's better to suffer than to have not lived.

ACHILLES What are you saying—that this is life? . . . Oh Patroclus. This is it. We had to witness the worst of things.

PATROCLUS Tomorrow I'll go out on the battlefield with you.

ACHILLES It's not my day yet.

PATROCLUS So I'll go alone. And I'll take your spear, just to embarrass you.

ACHILLES I hadn't been born when they took down the ash tree. I'd like to see the clearing where it stood.

PATROCLUS Come to the battlefield and you'll see it's worthy of you. So many enemies, so many tree stumps.

ACHILLES But the ships are not in flames yet.

PATROCLUS I'll take your armor and your sword. Your strength will be in my arms. And I'll be untouchable. Like a game.

ACHILLES You really are just a drunk little boy.

PATROCLUS When you ran with the Centaur, Achilles, you'd think about your memories. And you were no more immortal than you are tonight.

ACHILLES Only the gods see the future and live. But you are playing with fate.

PATROCLUS Drink more with me now. Then maybe tomorrow in Hades, I'll be saying the same thing to you.

THE ROAD

Oedipus & a mendicant

We all know it wasn't until after defeating the Sphinx and marrying Jocasta that Oedipus found out who he really was from the same shepherd who'd rescued him on Mount Cithaeron. Thus fulfilling the prophecy that he would kill his father and marry his mother. Horrified, Oedipus blinded himself, left Thebes, and took to the open road, where he died.

OEDIPUS. I'm not like other people, my friend. Fate has condemned me. I was born to rule. I grew up in the mountains. I walk in the dust and am stirred by the sight of a mountain or a tower, or a city in the distance. I never knew I was chasing my own fate. Now I can't see anything anymore and mountains are just work. Everything I do was destined. Get it?

MENDICANT I'm old, Oedipus, and all I've ever seen is destiny. But don't you think there are others—like the enslaved, crippled, and hunchbacked—who would have loved to be King of Thebes, like you?

OEDIPUS You've got to understand, my friend, my destiny is not about losing something. I'm not scared of the passing years or my ailing body. I want things to get worse. I'd be glad to lose it all—that's everyone's fate. But not mine, not Oedipus, the man who didn't know he was supposed to be a king.

MENDICANT I don't understand. You should be grateful for your privilege. You've had enough to eat and drink, had a bed to sleep in. It's worse when you're dead.

OEDIPUS That's not what I'm saying. The pain is from before—before I became anything, back when I might have been a man just like anyone else. But then there was destiny. I had to go to Thebes. I had to kill that old man. I had to father those children. Does any of it matter if it was all determined before you even existed?

MENDICANT It matters, Oedipus. You take what you've been given. The rest is up to the gods.

OEDIPUS There are no gods in my life. My lot is crueler than the gods. I was just naively trying, like everyone, to do better, to find some secret good in my days, something to soothe myself at night, the hope that tomorrow I'd do even more. Those are satisfactions even the most awful people get. But I was dogged by suspicion, muffled rumors, threats. This prophecy is all there's ever been, this sad declaration I just wanted to escape. I lived for years like a fugitive, always looking over my shoulder. I only ever dared believe in my own thoughts during a lull or after suddenly waking up. I have always been on guard. But I never ran away. Those were the moments that sealed my fate.

MENDICANT That's how it is for everyone, Oedipus. That's the meaning of fate. No doubt your situation has been awful.

OEDIPUS No! You don't understand, you don't understand, that's not it. I want it to be even worse. I want to be the most horrible person, someone so vile I would have wanted to do everything I did. Not subjected to it. Not pushed reluctantly into it. Who is Oedipus now, who are any of us, if even the darkest desires were already in our blood before we were born, and it was all as good as done?

MENDICANT Maybe there were some happy days for you. And I don't mean when you defeated the Sphinx and then all Thebes celebrated you, or when your first child was born, or when you took your throne. So you're done thinking about all of that, fine. But you've lived the same life as everyone else; you were young, you saw the world, you laughed and talked and enjoyed yourself—never unaware. The pleasure you took in things: going to sleep, waking up, walking down the street. You're blind now, fine. You used to be able to see.

OEDIPUS It would be foolish to deny that. I've had a long life. But what I'm trying to tell you is that I was born among you to rule. And when a man is sick, even the best fruit makes him sick and nauseous. Sickness is my destiny—the fear, the constant horror of doing exactly what I'm supposed to. I knew, I always knew, that I was like a squirrel—thinking I was climbing up and out, but really only spinning a wheel in a cage. And I wonder: Who was Oedipus?

MENDICANT A great man, a true leader—you could say that. They speak of you out on the road and at the gates of Thebes. Some people even left their homes, crossed Boeotia, saw the sea, and then, chasing your fate, went to Delphi to try the oracle. See? Your destiny was so extraordinary it affected other people. What of the man who never leaves his village, always does the same job, the same things every day, the same children, the same parties—and then he dies at the same age his father died of the same illness?

OEDIPUS I'm not like other men, I know. But I also think that even a servant or a fool would be disgusted by the crude pleasures of daily life if he really knew. Those unfortunate people who set out in search of my fate—maybe they were spared their own?

MENDICANT Life is big, Oedipus. The man you're talking to now—me—I was one of the unfortunates. I left my home and traveled Greece. I saw Delphi and I went to the sea. I hoped for an encounter, fortune, the Sphinx. I knew you were happy ruling Thebes. You were strong then. And even if I never found the Sphinx, or an oracle to speak about me, I'm happy with the life I lived. You were my oracle. You changed my destiny. To be a vagabond or king—what does it matter? We've both lived. The rest is up to the gods.

OEDIPUS But you'll never know if you were doing what you wanted to do . . . Sure, there's something uniquely human about the open road. The tortuous solitude is like an expression of that pain digging away at us. The pain is like a relief, like rain after muggy heat—it's quiet, peaceful, it seems to flow out of things, flow from the bottom of the heart. After all of destiny's deafening roar, peace and exhaustion are probably the only things we have that truly belong to us.

MENDICANT There was a time before we existed, Oedipus. Which means that the heart's desires, the blood, the awakenings, all came from nothing. I was about to say that even your determination to escape destiny is destined. We didn't make our own blood. Let alone know it and truly live—according to the oracle.

OEDIPUS As long as you're seeking, my friend, then yes. You were lucky you never found it. But the day comes when you go back to Cithaeron, and you forget all about everything, the mountain brings back your childhood, and you'll look at it every day and if you're lucky you'll climb it. Then someone will tell you that you were born up there and everything crumbles.

MENDICANT I see, Oedipus. But everyone has a childhood mountain. And for however long you wander, you end up on your path. That's where we are formed.

OEDIPUS It's one thing to talk and another to suffer, my friend. Though talking of course soothes something in the heart. Talking is a little like walking these roads the way we do, day and night, without a destination. We're nothing like the young men out seeking their fortune. You've talked a lot and seen a lot. Do you really want to rule?

MENDICANT Who knows? All I know for sure is that I needed a change. You go looking for one thing and find another. That's destiny too. But talking helps us rediscover ourselves.

OEDIPUS Do you have family? Do you have anyone? I suspect you don't.

MENDICANT I wouldn't be who I am.

OEDIPUS It's funny how we run from our fellow man in order to understand him, and that the most honest conversations we have are happenstance, between two strangers. I should have lived like this back when I had sight—Oedipus, traveling the roads that run along the Phocis and Isthmus. Not climbing mountains or listening to prophets . . .

MENDICANT You're forgetting at least one encounter in all that you've said.

OEDIPUS Which one, my friend?

MENDICANT The one with the Sphinx, at the crossroads.

THE ROCK

Heracles & Prometheus

In the history of the world, the period called the Time of the Titans was populated by men, monsters, and by gods not yet organized on Olympus. There are those who think perhaps that there were only monsters then—assuming that a monster is intelligence locked up in the deformed body of a beast. Which introduces the possibility that monster killers—Heracles in particular—spilled the blood of their own brothers.

HERACLES Prometheus, I've come to set you free.

PROMETHEUS I know. I've been waiting for you. I wanted to thank you, Heracles. You had an awful time getting here. Though, you are fearless.

HERACLES You've had a worse time of it, Prometheus.

PROMETHEUS Are you really fearless? That's hard to believe.

HERACLES If fear is what keeps you from doing the thing you're supposed to do, then no—I've never felt it. But I am a man, Prometheus, I don't always know what I am supposed to do.

PROMETHEUS Man is made of fear and compassion. There is nothing else.

HERACLES Prometheus, you've got me standing here chatting while your torture continues. I've come to set you free.

PROMETHEUS I know, Heracles. I've known you since you were a little baby, before you were even born. But now I'm feeling like a person who suffered somewhere—in prison or exile, in some great danger—so much so that when the moment comes to leave the suffering behind, he doesn't know how to manage it.

HERACLES You don't want to get off this rock?

PROMETHEUS No, I do have to leave. Like I said, I've been waiting for you. But this moment feels heavy—I feel it like a mortal. The suffering has been terrible, you know.

HERACLES I can see that just by looking at you, Prometheus.

PROMETHEUS You suffer so much you want to die. You'll know this feeling too, one day, when you climb your own rock. But I can't die. Neither can you for that matter, Heracles, you can't die.

HERACLES What are you talking about?

PROMETHEUS You'll be taken up by a god. Well, rather, by a goddess.

HERACLES I don't know, Prometheus. But here, let me untie you.

PROMETHEUS You'll be like a child, so full of excitement that you'll forget all the inequity and struggle. You'll live in the sky and praise the gods for their generosity and wisdom.

HERACLES Don't we owe everything to them?

PROMETHEUS There is a much more ancient wisdom than theirs, Heracles. The world is old, older than this cliff. Even they know that. Every last thing has a destiny. These gods are young, almost as young as you are.

HERACLES But aren't you a god too?

PROMETHEUS I will be yet. That's destiny's plan. But I was a Titan once and lived in a world without gods. That existed too . . . Can you imagine such a world?

HERACLES A world of chaos and monsters, no?

PROMETHEUS Of men and Titans, Heracles. Of beasts and forests. Of the sea and sky. A world of battle and bloodshed that made you who you are. Every single god, even the most unfair and immoral, was a Titan first. There's nothing worthwhile in this world or the next that wasn't once Titan.

HERACLES It was a world of rocks.

PROMETHEUS All mortals have their rock—all of you. That's why I loved you. These gods don't know about this rock. They don't know how to laugh or cry. They look at destiny and smile.

HERACLES Those are the ones who nailed you.

PROMETHEUS The victor is always a god, Heracles. Ever since Titan-man fought and resisted, he's been able to laugh and cry. If they nail you, if you climb the mountain, that's all the victory destiny allows. We should be thankful for it. What is victory if not a gesture of compassion, the saving of others at your own expense? Everyone works for someone else under the law of destiny. Even me—if I'm freed today, I'll owe that to someone.

HERACLES I've had worse tasks than this, and I haven't even freed you yet.

PROMETHEUS I'm not talking about you. You're compassionate and brave. But you've already done your part.

HERACLES I haven't done anything, Prometheus.

PROMETHEUS You wouldn't be mortal if you knew your destiny. But you live in a gods' world. And the gods even took that from you. You've done everything and you still know nothing. Remember the centaur.

HERACLES The man-beast I killed this morning?

PROMETHEUS Monsters don't get killed. Not even the gods can kill them. The day will come when you think you've killed another monster, more horrendous than the last, but what you've really done is prepared your own rock. Do you know who you struck down this morning?

HERACLES The centaur?

PROMETHEUS It was Chiron, merciful and dear friend to Titans and mortals.

HERACLES Oh Prometheus . . .

PROMETHEUS Don't torture yourself over it, Heracles. We're all complicit. It's the law of the world that no one gets out without having blood shed for them. The same will be true for you on Mount Oeta. Chiron knew that.

HERACLES Are you saying he sacrificed himself?

PROMETHEUS Absolutely. The same way I knew that stealing fire would be my rock.

HERACLES Let me untie you. Then you can tell me everything about Chiron and Oeta.

PROMETHEUS I'm already untied, Heracles. The only way I could really be released was for someone else to take my place. And Chiron let you strike him down. Fate sent you. In this world, born of chaos, the laws of justice rule. Compassion, fear, and courage are just tools. Nothing doesn't come back around. The blood you spilled and will spill will lead you to Oeta to die your death. The blood of the same monsters you live to destroy. You'll mount a pyre made from the fire I stole.

HERACLES But I can't die. You just told me that.

PROMETHEUS The gods brought death into this world. You mortals fear death because you know gods are immortal. But they'll have their end. Everyone gets the death they deserve. Even the gods have an end.

HERACLES What do you mean?

PROMETHEUS Not everything can be explained. Just always remember that monsters don't die. What dies is the fear they stir in you. Same with gods. Once humans stop fearing them, they'll disappear.

HERACLES And the Titans will come back?

PROMETHEUS The rocks and the forests will not come back. They're already here. That which has been will be.

HERACLES But even you were in chains.

PROMETHEUS Listen, Heracles. We are nothing more than a name. And the world has its seasons, like the fields and the soil. The winter comes back, the summer comes back. Who can say the forest will die? Or that it will stay the same? You'll be Titans soon.

HERACLES Us, mortals?

PROMETHEUS You mortals or you immortals—it doesn't matter.

INCONSOLABLE

Orpheus & Baccha

Sex, intoxication, and blood always conjure the underworld, and compel any number of people with Chthonic beatitudes. But Orpheus of Thrace, singer, tourist in Hades, and victim—cut into pieces like Dionysus himself—was the most important one.

ORPHEUS That's how it went. We were following the path through the forest of shadows. We'd already left Lake Cocytus, the Styx, the boat, and the laments far behind us. You could just make out the glimmer of sky on the leaves. I felt the brush of her footsteps behind me. But I'd been down there a while and had that cold on me. I was thinking I'd have to return one day—that what had been, would be again. I thought of my life with her, what it was like before; that it was going to end again. That which has been, will be. I thought of that iciness, the emptiness I'd journeyed through and what she was carrying in her bones, marrow, and blood. Was coming back to life worth it? I was considering all that when I saw daylight's shimmer. And I said, "Make it end." I turned around. Eurydice disappeared like a candle going out. I heard just a gurgle, like a drowning mouse.

BACCHA What a strange story. I almost don't quite believe it. Around here, they say the gods and muses were fond of you. Many of us stood by you because we knew how in love you were, and how unhappy. You were so in love that you alone among men, passed through the gates of nothing. No. I don't believe you, Orpheus. It wasn't your fault that destiny betrayed you.

ORPHEUS What does destiny have to do with it? My destiny does not betray. It's ridiculous to think that after that whole journey, after facing the void, I would have turned around accidently or on a whim.

BACCHA They say you did it for love.

ORPHEUS You can't love a dead person.

BACCHA And yet you wept for her, looked for her everywhere, over mountains and hills, you went down into Hades. What was that about?

ORPHEUS You talk like a man. But if you were, you'd know that men have no idea what to do about death. The Eurydice I mourned was a season of life. I was looking for something very different when I was down there, not her love. I was looking for a past Eurydice doesn't know. I realized it while singing to the dead. I saw the shadows stiffen, their eyes grow empty, their wailing stopped, Persephone hid her face, and Hades, that shadowy force, leaned forward to listen like a mortal. I understood then that the dead don't exist anymore.

BACCHA You were consumed with sorrow. Who wouldn't want the past, Orpheus? Eurydice was about to be reborn.

ORPHEUS Only to die again. To carry the horror of Hades in her blood and tremble at my side day and night. You don't know nothingness.

BACCHA So you, who managed to conjure the past through song, you rejected and destroyed it? I don't believe you.

ORPHEUS Listen to me, Baccha. The only true past was in the song. Hades could only see himself when listening to me sing. But that past was disappearing, I could already feel it becoming a memory on that path—the past reeked of death. When I saw that first sliver of sky, I skipped like a little boy—happy and full of wonder. I skipped for myself, for the living world. The season I was looking for was in that sliver of sky. I didn't care at all about the woman following me. The past was the twilight, it was the song and the morning. So I turned around.

BACCHA How do you reconcile this, Orpheus? People were terrified when they saw you coming back. Eurydice was your life.

ORPHEUS Nonsense. When Eurydice died, she became something else. The Orpheus who went down into Hades wasn't a husband anymore, or a widower. The grief I felt was like the grief you feel for childhood, for a memory that makes you smile. That season is over. I wasn't seeking her through my tears, but myself. Destiny, if you will. I was listening to myself.

BACCHA But we followed you because we believed in your grief. You tricked us?

ORPHEUS Why can't you understand? My destiny does not betray. I was looking for myself. A person looks for nothing else.

BACCHA We aren't that complicated here. We believe in love and in death, and we cry and laugh with everyone. Our most joyous celebrations are those where blood flows. We women of Thrace aren't frightened of such things.

ORPHEUS It's all wonderful when seen from this side of life. But I've been among the dead and believe me, it's not worth it.

BACCHA You weren't always like this. You didn't used to talk about the void. Getting close to death makes us too much like gods. You were the one who said that ecstasy inverts life and death, making us more than human . . . You saw revelry.

ORPHEUS It's not blood that counts, little girl. I'm not shocked by ecstasy or blood. But it's hard to say what a man is. Not even you know that.

BACCHA You wouldn't be anything without us, Orpheus.

ORPHEUS I know, and I've said as much myself. But then, who cares? I was alone when I went down into Hades . . .

BACCHA You went down to find us.

ORPHEUS But I didn't find you. And I wanted something else entirely. Something I found when I came back into the light.

BACCHA You once serenaded Eurydice from the tops of the mountains . . .

ORPHEUS Time passes. The mountains are still here but Eurydice isn't. Such things have a name, that name is human. There's no point invoking the gods of revelry here.

BACCHA You invoke them too.

ORPHEUS A person does all sorts of things in life. He'll believe everything over time. He even believes that his blood runs through another's veins. Or that something that has happened can be undone. He believes he can break destiny with drunkenness. I know all of this and it doesn't mean anything.

BACCHA You don't know what to make of death, Orpheus, and yet all your thoughts are about death. Once upon a time our revelry made us immortal.

ORPHEUS And you all do enjoy a party. Everything is legitimate to someone who still doesn't know. It's essential for every single person to take a turn in their own hell. The orgy of my destiny ended in Hades—ended with singing as I do, of life and death.

BACCHA What do you mean about destiny not betraying?

ORPHEUS It means that it's inside you; it's your own thing—more in you than your own blood, beyond ecstasy's reach. There's not a god who can touch it.

BACCHA Be that as it may, Orpheus, we're not looking for a Eurydice, so why did we follow you into hell?

ORPHEUS Every time you invoke a god, you meet death. You go down into Hades to break something, to violate destiny. You don't defeat darkness, and you lose the light. It's as if we're obsessed here.

BACCHA You say nasty things . . . And so, you've lost the light too?

ORPHEUS I was almost lost, and I sang. It was in realizing that I found myself.

BACCHA Is that the best way to find yourself? There's an easier path of bliss and ignorance. A god is like a king between life and death. We abandon ourselves to ecstasy, we fall to pieces or are pulled apart. But then we're reborn, every time, and just like you we wake to the daylight.

ORPHEUS Don't talk about daylight, or about awakening. Few men understand. A woman like you wouldn't know what it is.

BACCHA Maybe that's why the women of Thrace follow you. You're a god to them. You came down from the mountains. You sing songs about love and death.

ORPHEUS Fool. At least I can talk to you. Maybe one day you'll be like a man.

BACCHA So long as the women of Thrace don't first—

ORPHEUS Say it.

BACCHA So long as they don't tear the god to pieces.

WOLFMAN

two hunters

For his inhumanity, Zeus turned Lycaon, King of Arcadia, into a wolf. But the myth doesn't say how or where he died.

FIRST HUNTER This isn't the first time we've killed something.

SECOND HUNTER But it's the first time we've killed a man.

FIRST HUNTER That's not our concern. The dogs rousted him. It's not our business to know who he was. Why worry about his name or some old stories? He was cornered under the rocks, torn to pieces and bloody, wallowing in the mud, teeth redder than his eyes. He died with his jaws clenched around that javelin as if it were a dog's throat. He had an animal's skin and an animal's heart. There hasn't been a wolf like that in these woods for a while.

SECOND HUNTER I do worry about that, his name. I was only a kid when I first heard about him. The stories they told were unbelievable—that as a man he tried to slit the throat of the King of Olympus. For sure his coat looked like dirty snow—he was old, a ghost, but his eyes were the color of blood.

FIRST HUNTER It's done now. We have to skin him and get back to the valley. What a feast they'll throw for us.

SECOND HUNTER We'll move out at dawn. There's not much for us to do now except warm ourselves at the fire. The hounds will watch over the corpse.

FIRST HUNTER It's not a corpse, it's a carcass. We have to skin him though, otherwise he'll be stiff as a rock.

SECOND HUNTER I wonder whether we should bury him after we've taken the skin. He was human once. Drain the animal blood into the mud and all that will be left is a pile of bones and flesh, like an old man or a baby.

FIRST HUNTER You're not wrong about the old man part. These mountains were still deserted back when he became a wolf. He was older than the old lichen on these tree trunks. Who can remember his name or who he was? He should have died a long time ago, if I'm being frank.

SECOND HUNTER But we can't leave his body unburied . . . He was Lycaon. He was a hunter like us.

FIRST HUNTER Any one of us could die out on these mountains, and no one but the rain, or the vultures, would ever find the body. He died badly for a true hunter.

SECOND HUNTER He defended himself with his eyes, like an old man. But deep down, you don't believe he was like you. You don't believe he had a name. If you did, you wouldn't want to insult his corpse because you'd know that he also disrespected the dead. He was evil and inhuman. There was a reason the King of Olympus turned him into a wolf.

FIRST HUNTER They say he ate his own.

SECOND HUNTER I know men who've done less, and may as well be wolves, even if they don't howl or make dens in the woods. And are you so sure that you don't sometimes feel like Lycaon yourself? The rest of us have days when if a god should call on us, we'd cry out and go after anyone standing in our way. The only thing saving us is that when we wake up, we've got these hands, this mouth, a voice. But he didn't have a way out. Lycaon left human eyes and hearths behind forever. At least he'll find peace now that he's dead.

FIRST HUNTER I don't believe he needed peace. What more peace could he have wanted? He could hide on the cliffs and howl at the moon. I've been in the forest enough to know wild beasts and these trees have no fear of the sacred. They don't look up, except to shake their fur, or yawn. There may even be something about them that makes them equal to the gods in the sky. Whatever they do, they're remorseless.

SECOND HUNTER The way you talk makes it seem like being a wolf is a higher destiny.

FIRST HUNTER I don't know if it's high or low, but have you ever heard of a plant or animal turning themselves into a person? No. These places are filled with men and women who've been chosen by a god to be turned into a bush, or bird, or wolf. And what he got for his wickedness, for his crimes, was that he got to live without blood on his hands, he got to live without hope or remorse. He got to forget he was human. Isn't that just like how a god feels?

SECOND HUNTER A punishment is a punishment, and those who inflict it have compassion for the wicked at least in the sense that they take away doubt and make destiny of remorse. If an animal forgets his past and lives only for the hunt and for death, all that's left over is his name and what he once was. Old Callisto is buried in these hills. Does anyone remember her crime? And yet the rulers of the sky punished her horrendously. It's said she was once a beautiful woman, and they turned her into a bear, growling and weeping, scared every night and just wanting to go home. An animal like that has no peace. And then, her son comes along and kills her with his javelin. The gods do nothing. Though some say they repented and turned her into a star cluster. But there was a body, and it was buried.

FIRST HUNTER What do you mean? I know the stories. It's hardly the gods' fault that Callisto never accepted her fate. She's like a person who gets sad at a banquet or drunk at a funeral. If I were a wolf, I'd be a wolf even when I was asleep.

SECOND HUNTER You don't know the way of blood. The gods don't add or take away anything. They just, with the slightest touch, nail you where you've landed. Everything you've craved and everything you've chosen marks your desitny. That's what becoming a wolf means. What remains is whatever was left behind, what remains is the old Lycaon.

FIRST HUNTER You're saying that, while being torn apart by hounds, Lycaon suffered like a man who would hunt with dogs?

SECOND HUNTER He was old, done for. You were the one who pointed out he couldn't defend himself as he was dying, voiceless, on the rocks. I thought of those old beggars who stop sometimes in front of the gates, while the dogs lunge and strain against their chains to get to them. The same thing happens down our way. You could say that he lived as a wolf but died as a man. You could see it in his eyes.

FIRST HUNTER And you think he cares about whether he's rotting in the ground like a man when the last thing he saw was men hunting him down?

SECOND HUNTER There is peace after death. A common fate. It means something to the living, to the wolf in all of us. We had to kill him. We should stick to tradition and let the gods deal with indignance. Let's go home without blood on our hands.

THE GUEST

Lityerses & Heracles

The Greeks loved to tell horror stories about the kingdoms of Phrygia and Lydia. Clearly everything seemed to happen in one of those two places—but that was in another, more ancient time.

No need to even say who lost the reaping battle.

LITYERSES Here it is, traveler, our fields. Just like you people, we always welcome foreigners into our homes. There's no leaving here. Now that you have eaten with us and drunk with us, our land will drink your blood. This coming year, the grain will grow strong and dense along the banks of the Maeander.

HERACLES Have you murdered many travelers passing through your fields?

LITYERSES A number, yes. But never someone of your strength and singular stamina. With your red hair and eyes like flowers—you'll invigorate this land.

HERACLES Who taught you this ritual?

LITYERSES It's what we've always done. If you don't feed the earth, you can't expect it to feed you.

HERACLES Sure, but your crops seem abundant this year, as tall as a reaper's shoulders. Whose throat did you slit?

LITYERSES We haven't had any visitors. We had to kill an old servant and a goat. It was thin blood and barely made an impression on the earth. You see how hollow this husk is? A body must first sweat and froth in the sun before being bled. That's why we have you reap and carry bales until the exhaustion is drained out of you, and only then, once your blood is purified and quivering with life, we'll cut your neck. You are so young and strong.

HERACLES And what do your gods think of this?

LITYERSES There are no gods over this land. There is only the earth, the Mother, goddess of the cave who sleeps, stirring only when she feels that first splatter of blood. You'll be in her cave tonight, foreigner.

HERACLES Do you Phrygians ever go down into the cave?

LITYERSES We come from there. We're in no rush to return.

HERACLES I see. And so that's why your gods need to be bathed in blood.

LITYERSES Oh traveler, these are not gods—it's the earth. Don't your people live on this earth?

HERACLES Our gods do not live in the ground. They rule the earth, the sea, forest, and sky. As the shepherd watches over his flock and the master commands his servants, our gods live apart from us, up on the mountain—the way thoughts live inside the eyes of the person speaking to you, or the way there are clouds in the sky. They don't need blood.

LITYERSES Oh foreigner, my guest, I don't understand you. The clouds, the cliffs, the caves—they all share the same name, and don't live separate from each other. What blood the Mother gave us, we return in sweat, in excrement, in death. You really aren't from around here, are you? Those gods of yours can't be much.

HERACLES They are a lineage of immortals. They conquered the forest, the earth, and its monsters. They drove people like you, people who spill blood to feed the soil, back into the cave.

LITYERSES So your gods do know what they're doing. They had to feed the earth too. Be that as it may, you're too hearty to have been born from a hungry earth.

HERACLES Come on then, Lityerses, shall we reap?

LITYERSES You are an odd guest. No one has ever stood before these fields and made such a suggestion. Aren't you frightened of dying among the bales? Or are you hoping to escape through the furrows, like a quail or a squirrel?

HERACLES If I've understood you correctly, this is not death but a return to the Mother—a gift from a guest. All these peasants toiling away on the field, they will celebrate the person offering blood for them with prayers and song. It seems like a great honor.

LITYERSES Thank you, my guest. I can assure you the servant whose throat we slit last year didn't talk that way. He was old and tired, but we still had to bind him, and even then, he kept struggling, even as the scythes were already upon him, so that by the time he fell, he'd lost all his blood.

HERACLES It will go much better this time, Lityerses. Tell me, how exactly do you kill the unlucky man?

LITYERSES We cut him up while he's still alive and then scatter his parts around the fields to soak the Mother. We preserve the bloody head and wrap it in leaves and flowers, then at a certain point during the celebration, we throw it into the Maeander. As I said before, the Mother is not just soil, but also water and sky.

HERACLES You are very knowledgeable, Lityerses. It's not for nothing you're lord of the fields here in Celaenae. Tell me, do they kill a lot of people in Pessinus too?

LITYERSES Everywhere the sun shines, traveler, there is killing. Our crops don't thrive unless the soil's been soaked. The earth is alive. It needs nourishment.

HERACLES But tell me, why do you need to kill an outsider? This earth, the cave you emerged from, wouldn't it rather receive tribute from those closest to it? As you, for example, might prefer eating bread and drinking wine you've grown yourself?

LITYERSES I like you, traveler, you take our well-being to heart as if you were one of us. But think about why we toil and endure this terrible work. We are trying to live, right? And so, we should be the ones who live, so that we can enjoy the fruits of our labor. You're not a farmer.

HERACLES Yet, wouldn't it be better to figure out how to end the killing, so that everyone, whether foreign or native, can eat? If only there were a way to have one last sacrifice, someone whose blood would be enough to feed the earth, sky, and the sun's power over this land, forever.

LITYERSES It's obvious you don't work the land. Don't you know that the earth renews every solstice, and everything expires when the year turns?

HERACLES But there must be someone on this land who's been nourished by it for generations, who's drunk the juice of every season, someone whose blood is so rich, strong, and generous that it can replenish the earth for all time?

LITYERSES You make me laugh, stranger. I might suspect you're talking about me! I'm the only one in Celaenae whose forefathers have always lived here. I'm master of this land, and you know it.

HERACLES In fact, I was talking about you. We should reap, Lityerses. I travelled all the way from Greece to work for this blood. Today we reap. And tonight you return to the cave.

LITYERSES You want to kill me on my own field?

HERACLES I want to fight you to the death.

LITYERSES Do you even know how to handle a scythe, stranger?

HERACLES Don't you worry, Lityerses. Let's get to it.

LITYERSES You certainly do have strong arms.

HERACLES Let's get to it.

THE FIRES

Two shepherds

Even the Greeks practiced human sacrifice. Every rural society has done so. And all societies were rural once.

SON The whole mountain burns.

FATHER That's the idea. But Mount Cithaeron will be something different tonight. The animals graze too high up this year. Have you herded them?

SON No one will see our bonfire.

FATHER All that matters is that we light it.

SON There are more bonfires than stars.

FATHER Put on the log.

SON It's done.

FATHER Zeus, accept this offer of milk and sweet honey; we are poor shepherds and these flocks aren't ours to offer. May this burning fire keep trouble away, and as plumes of smoke spread over the fire, so may we be covered by rain clouds . . . Make it steam now, son. Just as long as they're killing a calf on one of the big farms. If it rains, it rains everywhere.

SON Over there, Father, are those stars or bonfires?

FATHER Pay attention over here. You have to send the vapor toward the sea. Rain comes from the sea.

SON Rain travels great distances, right father? Does it really rain everywhere when it rains? Even in Thespiae? Even in Thebes? They don't have any sea there.

FATHER But they have pastures, silly boy. They need wells. They are lighting fires tonight too.

SON And beyond Thespiae? Even farther away? Where a person could walk day and night and still be between two mountains? I've heard it never rains up there.

FATHER There are bonfires everywhere tonight.

SON But why isn't it raining yet? All the bonfires are lit.

FATHER It's a celebration, my boy. If it rained, the fires would go out. And what good would that do? It'll rain tomorrow.

SON So it's never rained while the bonfires were going?

FATHER Who knows? They've been lighting fires since before you were born, since even before I was born. It's always on the same night. I did hear it rained once on the fire.

SON Really?

FATHER But people were better off back then—even the sons of kings were shepherds. The whole world was a barnyard in those days. The ground was swept and clean, and everyone obeyed King Athamas. People worked and lived their lives and there was no reason to hide young goats from the landowners. They say there was a miserable heat wave one year, the pastures and wells all dried up and then people died. The bonfires didn't do any good. So Athamas sought counsel. But he was old and was under the influence of his young new bride. She filled his head with the idea that he needed to save face, not show any weakness. Sure, they prayed and spritzed water. Sure, they killed a calf and an ox . . . quite a few oxen. What happened next? Nothing. So, they decided to offer their children. Get it? Not her children, though, obviously not—she didn't have any—but the sons of the king's first wife, two young men who worked the fields all day long. That fool Athamas went with it. He sent for the boys. But those boys knew—one does—the children of kings aren't stupid, and so they took off. When they left, the clouds disappeared after them—the first clouds that a god sent over when he first heard about the situation. Then that witchy woman was quick to say, "See? We had the right idea. The clouds were there; so, we still have to spill blood." So, the people decided to round up Athamas and burn him.

They built and lit the fire; then brought out Athamas, bound and covered with flowers like a sacrificial bull. Just as they were about to throw him on the fire, the weather broke. Thunder! Lightning! The rain of the gods poured down. The crops came back to life. The rain drenched the fire, and Athamas, good soul that he was, forgave everyone, even his wife. Watch out for women, my son. You're more likely to catch a serpent than a snake.

SON What about the king's sons?

FATHER They were never heard from again. But two young men like that probably found something better to do.

SON If everyone was so good back then, why did they want to burn two boys alive?

FATHER You dunce, you're not comprehending what drought brings! I've been through them, and so has your grandfather. It's nothing like winter. Winter is difficult, but we know how to store the harvest. A drought, no. A drought burns. Everything dies. Thirst and starvation change a person. Take someone who hasn't eaten, and you get a brawler. Think about those people—everyone got along, everyone had a piece of land, and they were used to living well and being good. But you dry up their wells, scorch the crops, and everyone is starving and thirsty. People turn into animals.

SON They were wicked.

FATHER No more wicked than we are. We're ruled by the drought and no rain can free us from that.

SON I don't like the bonfires anymore. Why do the gods need them? Did they really used to burn people alive?

FATHER They took it slow, burning the lame, the lazy, the insane. Anyone who wasn't any use, they burned. Anyone who stole crops. Either way, the gods were satisfied. For better or worse, it rained.

SON I don't understand why that would make the gods happy. It rained anyway. What about Athamas? They put out that fire.

FATHER See, the gods are masters. Just like the masters, they don't want to see one of their own burn. They help each other out. But no one helps us. It doesn't matter to the gods whether it's nice out or it rains. We light fires now and say it brings rain. What does that matter to the masters? Have you ever seen them come out to the fields?

SON No, I guess not.

FATHER And so, once upon a time, lighting a bonfire was enough to make it rain, maybe you add a vagabond to the fire to save the crops. How many masters' houses need to burn, how many of them need to be cut down on the streets or in town squares before the world gets better and we can speak freely?

SON What about the gods?

FATHER What do they have to do with anything?

SON Didn't you say that gods and masters go hand in hand? They are all masters.

FATHER We'll slay a goat. What to do? We'll kill the vagabonds and anyone who steals from us. We'll make a pyre.

SON I wish it were tomorrow already. The gods frighten me.

FATHER That's a good thing. We need to keep the gods on our side. It's no good at your age not to think about these things.

SON I don't want to think about them. The gods are unjust. There's no good reason to burn people alive.

FATHER If it weren't this way, there'd be no gods. What would you do with yourself if you didn't work? Before the masters, when life was fair, you had to kill someone every now and then for the gods' pleasure. That's just their way. But they don't need as much these days. There are a lot of us in bad shape, and they get what they need just watching.

SON They're lazy bums too.

FATHER Lazy bums. You got that right.

SON What did they say while they were burning to death? The crippled children? Did they scream?

FATHER It's not the screaming so much. It's who's screaming that counts. Cripples and bad guys haven't done anything worthwhile. But it's a little worse when a hardworking man with a family watches some lazy bum get fat. That's injustice.

SON I can't stand still and think about bonfires from the old days. Look over there, how many of them are lighting up.

FATHER They didn't really burn a child on every fire. Could you imagine? It's like now, with the goat. If one person makes it rain, it rains for everyone. One man per mountain or village was enough.

SON I don't want to. Don't you understand. I don't want to. It's a good thing the masters consume us to the bone—we're so unfair to each other. The gods should watch us suffer. We're all evil.

FATHER Wet those branches now and make the water steam. You're naive. As if you're the only one who can talk about fairness and injustice. Over in the direction of the sea, dummy. Oh Zeus, accept this offering . . .

THE ISLAND

Calypso & Odysseus

We all know Odysseus was shipwrecked on his journey home and for nine years lived on the island of Ogygia—deserted, but for the ancient goddess Calypso.

CALYPSO We're not that different, Odysseus. You want to live on an island and so do I. You've already seen what there is to see, been through everything. Maybe one day I'll tell you all I've been through. We're both so tired from these big lives we've lived. Why go on? Does it really matter you didn't intend to stop on this island? Nothing ever happens here—it's a speck of dirt and a horizon. You could live here forever.

ODYSSEUS An immortal life.

CALYPSO An immortal accepts the moment, knows nothing of tomorrow. But, if that's the word you want to use, fine. Are you really at that point?

ODYSSEUS I had thought an immortal was someone who wasn't scared of death.

CALYPSO And someone who doesn't hope to live. Surely, you're practically there. You've suffered so much too. I don't understand your obsession with getting home. You're restless. Why do you go out to the headland alone and talk to yourself?

ODYSSEUS Would you be sad if I left tomorrow?

CALYPSO You want to know too much, my dear. Let's just say that I'm immortal. As for you, if you can't let go of your memories and dreams, if you can't let go of your obsessions and accept the horizon, you'll never be free of the destiny you know looms.

ODYSSEUS It's always about accepting some horizon. To what end?

CALYPSO Rest your mind and be still, Odysseus. Haven't you ever wondered why we want to rest too? Haven't you ever wondered where all the old gods go after the world's forgotten them? Why they sink into time like rocks in the dirt? Those old gods are eternal too. And what about me? Who is Calypso?

ODYSSEUS I asked you if you were happy.

CALYPSO That's not it, Odysseus. This air, the air on this deserted island that vibrates with the crashing waves and calling birds—it's empty. There's nothing to regret in such emptiness. Listen. Don't you also sometimes hear that silence, the stopping, like the trace of an ancient conflict and a presence that's disappeared?

ODYSSEUS So you go out to the headlands to talk to yourself too?

CALYPSO I'm telling you it's silence. Remote. Almost dead. What once was and will never be again. Back in the old world of the gods, a single gesture of mine was destiny. The names they called me inspired terror, Odysseus. The earth and sea obeyed me. Then I got tired; time passed; I stopped wanting to move. Some of us resisted the new gods, I let those names of mine sink into time, and then everything got quiet and remained the same; it just wasn't worth it to fight over the fate of new gods. I found my horizon and learned why the old gods hadn't been fighting alongside us.

ODYSSEUS Weren't you immortal?

CALYPSO I am, Odysseus. I don't hope to die. I don't hope to live. I accept this moment. It's the inversion of what's in store for mortals like you—the aging and regret. Don't you want to surrender to this island with me?

ODYSSEUS I would, if I actually believed you've surrendered. But you lord over all this, and yet still need me, a mortal, to help you endure it.

CALYPSO It goes both ways, Odysseus. Silence isn't real unless it's shared.

ODYSSEUS The fact that I'm here today isn't enough for you?

CALYPSO You're not here with me. You won't accept the horizon of this island. And you're not resisting regret.

ODYSSEUS My regrets are a living part of me, the same way your silence is for you. What's changed for you since the time when the earth and sea obeyed you? You've realized you're alone and tired, and that no one remembers all your names. Nothing was taken away. This was what you wanted.

CALYPSO What I am is almost nothing, my dear. Almost mortal, almost a shadow—like you. This is a long sleep, and no one knows when it started. You came to this sleep like a dream. I fear the dawn, the awakening. If you leave, that's the awakening.

ODYSSEUS Who's speaking now, you, the goddess?

CALYPSO I fear waking up the way you fear death. Sure, I was dead once, I know that now. There is nothing left of me on this island, but the voice of the sea and the wind. No, it wasn't suffering. I slept. But then you arrived and brought a different island with you.

ODYSSEUS I've been seeking home for too long. You've no idea what it's like to see land—just ahead if you squint—and every time, it's just a mirage. I can't simply stop moving and accept this horizon.

CALYPSO And yet, Odysseus, you men always say that it's wrong to look for what's been lost. The past doesn't repeat itself. Nothing defies the passing of time. You've seen the ocean, monsters, Elysium, will you recognize your houses, your own home?

ODYSSEUS You are the one who said I carry the island in me.

CALYPSO Oh, it's changed. Lost. Just silence. The echo of the waves against the rocks, a faint mist. No one can share that with you. Those houses will be like the faces of old people. Your words will mean something different from theirs. You will be more alone than you were out at sea.

ODYSSEUS Then at least I'll know it's time to stop.

CALYPSO It's not worth it. If you don't stop right now and here, you will never be able to stop. Whatever you do next will be what you always do. If you want to break away from the shackles of fate, you need to get off the road. Let yourself sink into time . . .

ODYSSEUS I am not immortal.

CALYPSO You could be if only you listened to me. What is eternal life, after all, if not accepting that these moments come and go? The shiver, the pleasure, death—they have no other purpose. What have all your restless mistakes added up to?

ODYSSEUS If I knew the answer, I would have already stopped. But you are forgetting something.

CALYPSO Tell me.

ODYSSEUS Everything I seek, I hold in my heart, like you.

THE LAKE

Virbius & Diana

Hippolytus, chaste hunter of Troezen, died a horrible death for his disrespect of Aphrodite. But Diana revived him and whisked him away to Italy (Esperia), to the Alban Hills, where she adopted him into her cult and renamed him Virbius. Virbius had children with the nymph Aricia. For the ancients—thinking of the Odyssey—the West was the land of the dead.

VIRBIUS I wanted to tell you how happy I am I came here. This lake seems like the ancient sea. And I was happy to live your life, to be dead to everyone else, to serve you in the forest and in the hills. The wild animals here, the peaks, and the locals know nothing but you. This is a place without a past; it is a village of the dead.

DIANA Hippolytus . . .

VIRBIUS Hippolytus is dead. You named me Virbius.

DIANA Don't you mortals ever forget your lives, Hippolytus, not even in death?

VIRBIUS Listen. As far as anyone is concerned, I'm dead and I serve you. When you pulled me out of Hades and gave back the light, I asked for nothing more than to be able to move, breathe, and worship you. You placed me here, where both the earth and sky glitter, where everything is fragrant and healthy, and everything is new. Even nighttime is young and deep here, much more so than in my homeland. Time doesn't pass here. Memories are not made. And you alone rule.

DIANA You are saturated with memories, Hippolytus. But, allowing for a moment that this is the land of the dead, what else does a person do in Hades besides revisit the past?

VIRBIUS I told you, Hippolytus is dead. This lake that looks like the sky recognizes no one named Hippolytus. If I weren't here, this place would be exactly the same. Like an imaginary land seen from a distance through the clouds. Once back home—when I was still a child—I thought that on the other side of the mountains, far away where the sun goes down, that was where the newborn morning lived, and if I could just get there, I could hunt and play all the time. Then a slave said to me, "Be careful what you wish for, little one. The gods always deliver." That place was here. I never realized that what I wanted was death.

DIANA Yet another memory. Why are you complaining?

VIRBIUS Oh wild one, I don't know. It seems like only yesterday I opened my eyes here. I know a lot of time has passed, and these mountains, this water, these big trees are silent and still. Who is Virbius? Am I different from that boy who woke every morning and went right back to playing as if time didn't pass?

DIANA You are Hippolytus, the boy who died to follow me. And now you live beyond time. You don't need memories. With me, you live in the moment, like the hare, like the deer, like the wolf. We flee, we always chase. This isn't the land of the dead, but rather the living twilight of a forever tomorrow. You don't need memories because this is the life you've always known.

VIRBIUS And yet it's much more alive here than it was back home. Everything has a radiant light and the sun—it's like it's coming from within, a vitality that could be described as unaffected by the days. What is this land of Esperia to the gods?

DIANA No different from all the other lands under the sky. We don't live in the past or in the future. For us, every day is like the first. What seems like great silence to you is our sky.

VIRBIUS But I've lived in places you care more about. I hunted on Mount Didymus, raced on the beaches of Troezen—places that are poor and wild like me. Yet in this unhuman silence, this life beyond life, I've never held my breath. What creates this solitude?

DIANA You are a child. A place where man has never been, is always the land of the dead. Others will come from your sea and islands and think they've crossed over into Hades. There are other lands, even farther away . . .

VIRBIUS Other lakes, other mornings like this one. The water is bluer than sloe berries in the leaves. I feel like a shadow in the shadows of trees. The more this sun warms me and the land feeds me, the more I feel like I'm melting into buzzing and droplets, into the call of the lake and the growling forest. There is something faraway behind the tree trunks, in the stones, in my own sweat.

DIANA These are the ravings of your childhood.

VIRBIUS I'm no longer a child. I know you and I've come here from Hades. My homeland is as far away as the clouds up there. I move among the trees and things as if I were a cloud.

DIANA You are happy, Hippolytus. If man can be happy then you are.

VIRBIUS The boy I was, the one who died, is happy. You saved him and I'm grateful. But this reborn fugitive, your slave, the one who watches over your oak trees and your forests—he is not happy because he doesn't even know if he exists. Who speaks to him? Who answers him? How is today more than his yesterday?

DIANA Ah, is that all? You want some company?

VIRBIUS You know what I want.

DIANA That's what mortals always end up asking for. Is it something in your blood?

VIRBIUS You're asking me about blood?

DIANA There's so much savoring in spilled blood. How often I've watched you turn over a deer or a wolf, slit its throat and bathe your hands. It's why I liked you. But I'm less familiar with the other blood, the blood that fills your veins and ignites your eyes. I know that to you, it's life and destiny.

VIRBIUS I shed that once already. And that restless, lost feeling is proof, on this day, that I'm alive. The lush plants and the light off the lake, none of it is enough for me. These things might as well be clouds, eternal wanderers of dawn and dusk, guardians of the horizon, characters in Hades. Other blood is the only thing that can soothe my blood. Blood that is restless, then satisfied.

DIANA You want to slaughter something, is that what I'm to understand?

VIRBIUS You are not wrong, wild one. Back when I was Hippolytus, I slaughtered wild animals. It was what I wanted. But here, in the land of the dead, even animals slip from my grasp like clouds. I think it's my fault. But I need the closeness of warm blood like my own. I need a voice and a destiny. Wild one—allow me this.

DIANA Consider it well, Virbius-Hippolytus. You've been happy.

VIRBIUS It doesn't matter, my lady. I've seen my own reflection in the lake too many times. I don't want to be happy, I want to live.

WITCHES

Circe & Leucothea

Odysseus had been warned before he met her that Circe was dangerous, and he received protection from her spells and the touch of her magic wand. The sorceress—an ancient Mediterranean goddess fallen from favor—had long known destiny would bring an Odysseus to her. Homer didn't track that part of the story as much as we wish he had.

CIRCE Believe me, Leucò, I didn't get it in the moment. Sometimes a mistake in the potion causes amnesia. But I did touch him. The truth is I'd been waiting for him for so long I stopped thinking about it. And then, as soon as I realized what was happening—when he lunged at me, hand on his sword—I wanted to smile. I was so happy, and disappointed too. I had thought maybe I could even resist, escape fate. But then I thought, This is Odysseus—a man who wants to go home. I was already planning how to send him off. My dear Leucò. He waved that sword around—so brave and ridiculous, the way only men know how to be—and I couldn't help but smile and square off, as I do with men, and then I acted surprised and backed away.

I felt like a child—the way we laughed and laughed when we were little girls after they told us what being grown up would be like. Everything unfolded like a dance. He grabbed my wrists and raised his voice. I got so flushed, Leucò, and yet I was pale. I grabbed his knees and started my spell: "Who are you? What land do you come from . . ." Poor man, I thought. He has no idea what's in store for him. He's a big, handsome man with curly hair. What a stupendous pig, what a marvelous wolf he would have made.

LEUCOTHEA You told him all this during the year he spent with you?

CIRCE Don't talk about destiny with a man, my child. They're sure they said everything there is to be said about destiny when they called it the iron chain, the fatal decree. They call us the fatal ladies, you know?

LEUCOTHEA They don't know how to laugh.

CIRCE True. Though some of them do know how to laugh at the prospect of fate; others know to laugh once it's over; but they really need to laugh while it's happening, otherwise they die. They can't joke about divinity; they don't know how to talk about themselves the way we do. Their life is so short, they refuse to do things they've already done or see things they've already seen.

As for him, Odysseus the brave, if I were to talk to him this way, he'd have trouble understanding and start thinking about Penelope.

LEUCOTHEA What a bore.

CIRCE Yes, but I get it. He didn't need to laugh when he was with Penelope. With her, everything, even daily meals, were significant and unpredictable—that's how they prepared themselves for death. You've no idea how much death fascinates them. Sure, dying is their destiny, they practice it, it's a known quantity, but they're fooling themselves when they think it changes anything.

LEUCOTHEA So why wouldn't he want to be turned into a pig?

CIRCE He didn't even want to be turned into a god, and you know how long Calypso begged him. The fool. That's the way Odysseus is—neither pig nor god, just a man, an extremely intelligent man, and fearless in the face of destiny.

LEUCOTHEA Tell me, my dear, did you actually like being with him?

CIRCE I think one thing, Leucò. None of us goddesses have ever wanted to become mortal, we never longed for it. And yet, it would be just the thing, something new to break the chain.

LEUCOTHEA Is that what you want?

CIRCE What do you think, Leucò? . . . Odysseus couldn't figure out why I smiled. He often couldn't even tell that I was smiling. There was one time I thought I'd explained why beasts are more like us immortals than man is—despite all that intelligence and bravery. An animal eats, has sex, and has no memory of it. Odysseus replied that he had a dog waiting for him back home. Poor dog—probably long dead. He told me its name. Can you believe the dog had a name?

LEUCOTHEA Men give us all names.

CIRCE Odysseus gave me a lot of names in bed. There was a new name every time. In the beginning, they were more like animal sounds—like a pig or a wolf. But then he realized the sounds were syllables that combined into a word. Then he called me by the names of all the goddesses, of our sisters, the names for the Mother, all names. It was as if he were fighting me, fighting fate. He wanted to name me, hold me, make me mortal. He wanted to break something. He had plenty of courage and intelligence, but he didn't know how to smile. He never knew the smiling of the gods, the smiling of those who know destiny.

LEUCOTHEA No man understands us or the beast. I've seen your men. Even after you turn them into wolves and pigs, they still growl like men. It's torture. They are coarse despite their intelligence. Do you toy with them a lot?

CIRCE I have fun. I have as much fun as I can. I was never meant to share my bed with another god, and as for men, Odysseus is the only one. Everyone else I touch turns into an animal, they swell with rage and come at me like that, like a beast. I'll take them. Their rage is no better or worse than a god's love. But with beasts, I don't have to smile. I feel them on me; then they escape back to their dens. I never lower my eyes.

LEUCOTHEA And Odysseus . . .

CIRCE I don't wonder who they might be . . . You want to know who Odysseus was?

LEUCOTHEA Tell me, Circe.

CIRCE One night he told me about when they arrived here on Aeaea, He described his men's fear, the sentinels standing on deck. He told me about camping out on the beach and lying there listening to the growling and roars. And then when daylight came, they saw a plume rising from the thicket and shouted with joy, because they recognized home in the smoke.

He told me all this with a smile—the way men smile—sitting by my side in front of the fire. He told me he wanted to forget where he was and who I was and that night he called me Penelope.

LEUCOTHEA He was that foolish?

CIRCE I was foolish too, my dear. I told him to cry.

LEUCOTHEA Imagine that.

CIRCE But he didn't cry. He knew Circe loves animals, and animals don't cry. He cried later. He cried the day I told him what a long journey he still had before him, and that at the Lake of Averno he'd go down into the underworld, and I told him about the total darkness of the ocean. Tears that clear the eyes and make you feel stronger. Even I get it. But then, that evening he told me about his childhood and his destiny, laughing mysteriously as he spoke, and he asked me to tell him about myself. Get it? He was laughing while he talked.

LEUCOTHEA I don't get it.

CIRCE He was laughing out loud, full-throated, but his eyes were full of memories. And then he asked me to sing. So, I went to the loom and sang, and my raspy voice formed the song of home and his childhood. I sweetened it. I was Penelope for him. He put his head in his hands.

LEUCOTHEA Who was laughing in the end?

CIRCE No one, Leucò. Even I was mortal that night. My name was Penelope. That was the only time I've ever looked at my fate and, without smiling, averted my gaze.

LEUCOTHEA This man loved a dog?

CIRCE A dog, a woman, his son, and a seafaring ship. And the countless cycle of days that never struck him before as destiny. He ran toward death, knowing what it was, and he made the world richer with his words and deeds.

LEUCOTHEA Oh Circe, I don't have your eyes, but I want to smile now too. You were naive. If you'd told him you lay down with wild animals, with wolves and boar, he would have succumbed. He would have turned animal too.

CIRCE I did tell him. But he just made a face and then after a moment said, "As long as they aren't my men."

LEUCOTHEA So he's jealous.

CIRCE Not jealous. He cared for them. He understood everything. Except for the laughter of gods. The day he wept on my bed, he wasn't crying out of fear, but because his last journey was written by fate—it was already known. "So why should I even do this?" he asked me, girding his sword and heading toward the shore.

I brought him the black lamb and his men wept, and he watched a flock of birds fly off. "They're heading out too," he said. "But they don't know what they're going to do. Whereas you, my lady, do know."

LEUCOTHEA That's all he said?

CIRCE That's it.

LEUCOTHEA Why didn't you kill him, Circe?

CIRCE I really am an idiot. Sometimes I forget what the rest of us know. Then I play like a child. As if all these same sorts of things happened to the great gods, to the Olympians, and happened in exactly the same way—inexorable but sudden and absurd. The thing I never predict is predictably what's been predicted—which is that I always know what I'll do and what I'll say, and so what I do say and do always seems new and surprising, like a game, like chess—the game Odysseus taught me. It's all rules and regulations but it's also beautiful and unexpected, with those little ivory pieces. He told me chess is a way of defying time.

LEUCOTHEA Too many things remind you of him. Instead of turning him into a wolf or a pig, you turned him into a memory.

CIRCE Man is mortal, Leucò. It's the only bit of immortality he has. The memory he carries and the memory he leaves. I am names and words. They smile at memories too. You should just accept it.

LEUCOTHEA You also use words.

CIRCE Don't worry, Leucò. I know my destiny.

BULL

Lelego & Theseus

We all know that Theseus, on his way back from Crete, somehow forgot to lower the black sails on his ship, signaling his death. Grief-stricken, Theseus's father threw himself into the sea, leaving the kingdom as inheritance. This is very Greek, as Greek as the repulsion for any sort of mystical monster cult.

LELEGO The hill over there, that's home, sir.

THESEUS There isn't any bit of land on the horizon that in this dusky light doesn't seem like our old hill.

LELEGO We once toasted the sunset over Mount Ida too.

THESEUS It's nice to come home and nice to leave. We should drink more, Lelego. We'll drink to the past. The greatness of everything left behind and everything rediscovered.

LELEGO The whole time we were on that island, you never talked about home. You had no regrets about what we left behind. You lived in the moment. Then

I watched you leave, the same way you'd left home, without looking back. Will you be thinking of the past tonight?

THESEUS We're alive, and we have this wine and the shores of home ahead of us. There are many things a person might consider on a night like this—even if by tomorrow wine and home shores won't be enough.

LELEGO What are you frightened of? It's almost as if you don't believe in your own return. Why don't we take down the black sails and dress the ship white? You promised your father.

THESEUS We have time, Lelego. Time tomorrow. I like these sails fluttering over my head, they're the same ones we flew when we were heading into danger, and none of you knew if you'd ever come back.

LELEGO But, you knew, Theseus?

THESEUS More or less . . . My hatchet never fails.

LELEGO Why do you hesitate?

THESEUS I'm not hesitating. I'm thinking about the people I ignored, the great mountain and who we were back on the island. I'm thinking of our last days in the kingdom, that palace with endless courtyards, and how the soldiers called me the Bull King. Remember? You become what you've killed on that island. I was starting to understand them. Then they told us about the grottos of the gods in the forests of Ida, where gods were born and died. Don't you get it, Lelego? They killed gods like they were animals on that island. And, if you kill a god, you become a god. Then we tried to climb Ida . . .

LELEGO Being away from home makes you brave.

THESEUS They spoke of such amazing things. The women, those tall, blonde women who spent the mornings sunbathing on the palace terraces and then would climb up to the groves on Ida where they'd hug the trees and the animals. Sometimes they stayed there.

LELEGO The women are the only brave ones on that island. You know that, Theseus.

THESEUS There's one thing I know. I prefer women to be at their looms.

LELEGO But there aren't any looms on the island. Everything is bought overseas. So, what are the women supposed to be doing?

THESEUS Not growing old in the sun thinking about gods. Not trying to find divinity in tree trunks or the ocean. Not chasing bulls. I used to think it was the fathers' fault, those clever merchants who dressed like women and liked to watch boys twirl around on bulls. But that's not it, or not only it. They have different blood. There was a time when Mount Ida was only for goddesses. One goddess. She was the sun, the trees, the sea. Men and gods alike turned into fools in her presence. When a woman escapes a man, and finds herself in the sun and among animals, it's not the man's fault. The blood gets damaged; it's chaos.

LELEGO Only you could say that. Are you thinking of the foreign woman?

THESEUS Her too.

LELEGO You're the captain, and whatever you do is right by us. Though she gave us the impression of being docile and obedient.

THESEUS Too docile, Lelego. Docile like grass or the sea. You look at her and see she's pliant, and she can't feel you. Like the groves on Ida, where you move forward with one hand on your hatchet, but then the silence becomes overwhelming and you have to stop. Like the panting of an animal lying in wait. Even the sun and air seem to be part of the ambush. You don't fight the great Goddess. You don't fight the earth . . . or its silence.

LELEGO I know all this as well as you. But the foreigner led you out of the labyrinth. She left her home. Which has nothing to do with hot blood or damaged blood. She left her own gods behind to follow you.

THESEUS But the gods didn't leave her.

LELEGO You also said they slaughter them up on Ida.

THESEUS Then the killer becomes the new god. Look Lelego, you can kill bulls and gods in a cave, but you can't kill the divinity in their blood. Ariadne had island blood too. I know it like I know the bull.

LELEGO You were cruel, Theseus. What do you think she said when she woke up, miserable?

THESEUS I know. Maybe she cried out. But for nothing. Invoked her country, the homes, and her gods. She's got the sun and the earth. Us foreigners are nothing to her now.

LELEGO She was beautiful, sir. She was like the earth and sun.

THESEUS And we're only men. I'm sure they'll send someone over to console her, some god in pain, some gentle and shadowy god, who's already tasted death and is tied to the apron strings of the great Goddess. Will it be a tree, a horse, a ram? Maybe a lake or a cloud? Anything goes in her sea.

LELEGO I don't know. Sometimes you talk like a child playing a game. You're in charge so we listen to you. Other times, you're old and cruel. One might say that some part of the island got into you.

THESEUS That's also possible. If you kill it, you become it. You don't think it, but we're coming from far away.

LELEGO You're not even warmed by the wine of our homeland?

THESEUS We aren't home yet.

IN FAMIGLIA

Castor & Pollux

The grievous events that plagued the House of Atreus are notorious. But we only need to keep a few generations in mind for our purposes here: Pelops was born to Tantalus. Atreus and Thyestes were born to Pelops. Menelaus and Agamemnon were born to Atreus. Agamemnon was the father of Oreste, who killed his mother. That Artemis of the wilderness and sea enjoyed a cult status in this family (consider the attempted sacrifice of Iphigenia by her own father) is something this writer has been long convinced of.

CASTOR Do you remember when we got her back from Theseus?

POLLUX It was worth it . . .

CASTOR She was just a little girl and I remember thinking while we were racing through the night how scared she must be on Theseus's horse in that forest being chased by us . . . We were naive.

POLLUX She's safe now.

CASTOR Now she has Phrygians and Dardanians protecting her. She's put a sea between us.

POLLUX We'll cross the sea.

CASTOR I'm done with it all, Pollux. It's not our business anymore. Now it's all the House of Atreus.

POLLUX We'll cross the sea.

CASTOR Keep convincing yourself of that, Poll-Poll. It's not worth it. Don't be naive. Leave the House of Atreus to its own future.

POLLUX But she's our sister.

CASTOR We should have known she wouldn't stay in Sparta. She's not the kind of woman who wants to live in the back of some palace.

POLLUX What else could she want, Castor?

CASTOR She doesn't want anything. That's the thing. She's the same little girl she was then. She is incapable of taking a husband or a house seriously. But it's useless to go after her. She'll come back to us one day, you'll see.

POLLUX It's anyone's guess now what bloody revenge the House of Atreus will seek. Those people can't tolerate an insult. They take their honor as seriously as the gods themselves.

CASTOR Nothing to do with the gods. That family has always eaten themselves alive. Starting with Tantalus, who lavishly served his son for dinner . . .

POLLUX So the stories are true?

CASTOR It's what you'd expect. People who live in fortresses in Sparta and Mycenae and have golden funeral masks, people who govern the sea by watching through an arrow slit, are capable of anything. Haven't you ever wondered why their women, our sister included, get more and more wild and ferocious? They spill blood, order it to be spilled. The best of them don't last. There's no Pelopidas among them—not a one who's died in his wife's arms. If such is an honor of the gods . . .

POLLUX But our other sister, Clytemnestra, is doing fine.

CASTOR Why don't we wait until the end of the story on that.

POLLUX If you knew all this, why did you consent to the marriage?

CASTOR I didn't consent. These things happen. Men marry the wives they deserve.

POLLUX What do you mean? Do the women deserve them? Is our sister to blame?

CASTOR Stop it, Pollux. No one listens to us. It's obvious that the men of Atreus always marry the same woman. We're her brothers, but maybe we just don't know who Helen really is. Theseus gave us the first clue. Then Atreus. Now Paris the Phrygian. It can't possibly be all coincidence. She's always going off with the same kind of man. It's becoming obvious that she's a type, and she has a type.

POLLUX Are you nuts?

CASTOR There's nothing nuts about it. It's their problem if they're losing their minds—and some of them, their necks too. The Tantalids are a lineage of sea kings who never leave home and love commanding from on high. Maybe they once explored the world. Surely Tantalus did. But then they shut themselves up with their women and piles of gold, got paranoid and unhappy, totally incapable of making an honest move, and their land is poor, but they feed off the sea, they have banquets, they're fat. Is it a surprise that they seek out strong, almost savage, women to lock up on the mountain with them. They always get them.

POLLUX I don't understand what our sister has to do with this or why you're saying that she was a perfect match for Paris or Theseus.

CASTOR Perfect for them, perfect for others—it doesn't matter, Poll-Poll. We're talking about the destiny of the House of Atreus. If they all act like a herd of wild horses, it's not ancient Hippodamia's fault, or even that of the daughters-in-law. You could say that the men of that family have all been the same man and they've sought the same woman. And found her. Starting with Hippodamia, daughter of Oenomaus, all the way down to our sisters, the women have all been forced to fight and defend themselves. Clearly that gives the men pleasure. They might not know it, but it does. They're a bloody, manipulative family. Fat tyrants. They need a woman to whip them into shape.

POLLUX You keep saying Hippodamia, Hippodamia. Even I know that Hippodamia spurred on the horses. But that has nothing to do with our sisters. Helen has the hands of a girl who's never held a whip. How can you compare them?

CASTOR We don't know much about women, Pollux. We grew up with her. To us, she will always be the little girl bouncing a ball. But you don't have to whip horses to feel wild and frenzied. All it takes is some attention from Menelaus, from a king of the sea.

POLLUX What did Hippodamia do that was so terrible?

CASTOR She treated men like horses. She got the charioteer to kill her father. She got Pelops to kill the charioteer. She birthed the murderous brothers and laid the path for a river of blood. And yet, she never fled her houses, no.

POLLUX Didn't you say it was Pelops's fault?

CASTOR I said that Pelops and his people all liked the same kind of women. Women who were their perfect matches.

POLLUX Helen isn't a killer, and she won't have someone killed.

CASTOR Are you sure of that, brother? Remember when we took her from Theseus—three horses galloping through the forest. If we didn't die, it was only because we were kids and we thought it was a game. But you're still asking how much blood is being spilled at the House of Atreus.

POLLUX But she isn't spurring on anyone . . .

CASTOR Do you believe Hippodamia incited the charioteer? She smiled at her servant and mentioned her father was keeping her for himself. She didn't even say she minded . . . One look is enough to instigate murder. Then, after Myrtilus realized he was being played by the son of Tantalus and wanted to cry out a warning, all Hippodamia had to do was tell her husband, "He knows about Oenomaus. Watch out for him." Those people revel in wordplay.

POLLUX So all women are killers?

CASTOR Not all of them. Some of them simply bow their heads and let life enslave them. But even those women get unhinged in the fortress. The House of Atreus kills and gets killed. They need to whip and be whipped.

POLLUX Our sister will be happy to get out of there.

CASTOR Do you believe that, brother? Remember Aerope, the wife of Atreus . . .

POLLUX Aerope was killed at sea.

CASTOR Not before having urged her lover to steal treasure. She was a woman driven mad by the fortress. A woman who could have had an easy life of lust, growing fat along with her lover. But her lover was Thyestes and her husband was Atreus. They chose her. They wouldn't let her save herself. They unleashed her too. That family hungers for rage.

POLLUX Are you saying that they're going to kill our sister for adultery? That she's lustful too?

CASTOR Were that so, Pollux, were that so. But lust isn't for everyone. Not for someone who marries a descendent of Atreus. Don't you get it, those guys lust for a violent embrace, the beating and the blood? They wouldn't know what to do with a humble, obedient woman. They need to gaze into cold, murderous eyes, eyes that don't look away. Just like Hippodamia's arrow slits.

POLLUX Our sister has this look . . .

CASTOR They need a cruel virgin. One who can cross mountains. Every woman they marry is that for them. They'll feast on her children, they'll slaughter them . . .

POLLUX That's all in the past.

CASTOR They'll never stop, Pollux.

THE ARGONAUTS

Jason & Melite

Pindar also writes about the temple of Acrocorinth, overseen by Hierodules. Even if we didn't already know from the stories, we might easily assume that young monster chasers, including Theseus of Athens, had trouble with women. Euripides recounts the story of Medea one of the most horrific women, with her jealousy, sorcery, and infanticide at length and with fervor in his beloved play.

JASON Go ahead and open the curtains, Melite. I can feel the breeze that's lifting them. Even Jason wants to see the sky on a morning like this. Tell me about the ocean; tell me what's happening in the port, out on the water.

MELITE Oh King Jason, it's so lovely from up here. The docks are filled with people, a ship is pulling out from among the other boats. It's so clear, I can see its upside-down reflection. If you only could see the flags and festoons. So many people. They're even climbing the statues. The sun is in my eyes.

JASON Your friends must have come to see them off. Can you see them, Melite?

MELITE I can't tell, there are so many people. And all the sailors up on the rigging, teeny tiny, waving back.

JASON Wave to them, Melite. It must be the Cyprus ship. They'll pass through all your islands. The fame of Corinth and its temple means they'll even be talking about you.

MELITE What would they say about me on the islands? Who do you think even remembers me?

JASON There's always someone to remember young people. It's nice to think about someone young. What about the gods, aren't they young? That's why everyone remembers them and why we're jealous of them.

MELITE We serve them, King Jason. And I serve the goddess too.

JASON Surely there will be someone, a traveler or sailor, who will go up to the temple to be with you and you alone. Someone whose tribute is only for you. I'm old and I can't climb that high, but there was a time in Iolcus, before you were even born, that I would have climbed higher than a mountain to be with you.

MELITE You command and we all obey . . . Oh, the ship is unfurling its sails! They're all white. Come and see.

JASON Stay at the window, Melite. I'll watch you watching the ships. It will be like we're watching them catch wind together. I'd shiver in the morning air. I'm old. I'd see too much if I looked down there.

MELITE The ship is shifting in the sunlight. It's flying now! Like a dove.

JASON And it's only going to Cyprus. Ships are setting off for the open sea from Corinth now and from the islands. Time was, there was nothing here. We were the first to sully it. You weren't even born yet. It seems so long ago.

MELITE I can hardly believe it, my king, no one ever dared cross?

JASON Some things have a virginity about them, Melite, that stirs more fear than daring. Consider how terrifying the mountain summits are, consider the echo.

MELITE I'll never climb to the top of a mountain. But I can't believe that anyone is frightened of the ocean.

JASON Actually we never made it. We took off from Iolcus on a morning like this one and we were all young and had the gods on our side. What a thrill to set out, not a thought for what was to come. Then the wonders started. It was a younger world, the days were all bright mornings, the nights a darkness so dense anything could happen. There was always a new marvel—waterfalls, monsters, men or cliffs. Some of us disappeared, others died. Every docking meant a funeral. And every morning the sea was even more beautiful, more virginal. The days were full of expectation. Then the rains came, the fog came, and the sea churned black.

MELITE Nothing new.

JASON The danger wasn't the sea. We came to understand, from one landing to the next, that the long journey had aged us. We were stronger and had grown detached—we were like gods, Melite—which was exactly what drew us to everything deadly. We came ashore at Phasis, on the crocus fields. I was so young then and looking at my fate.

MELITE We lower our voices in the temple when we talk about you all.

JASON It makes you laugh sometimes, I know. Corinth is a happy city. And I know people say, "When is that old guy going to stop going on about his gods? They're all dead by now, anyway, just like the others." Corinth wants life.

MELITE We talk about the sorceress, King Jason, the woman only a few have met. Tell me about her.

JASON Everyone knows a sorceress, Melite, except in Corinth where the temple teaches laughter. But the rest of us, the old and the dead, have all met a sorceress.

MELITE What about yours, King Jason?

JASON We raped the sea, we destroyed monsters, we tromped through the crocus meadows—that golden glitter in the forest—yet some of us died from dark arts, and others because of a spell or the passion of a sorceress. And some of us now —talking to you—we're old, and saw our children murdered by their mad mother.

MELITE They say she isn't dead, my king, that her spells defied death.

JASON That's her destiny and I don't envy it. She inhaled death and spat it out. Maybe she's gone home.

MELITE How could she hurt her own children? She must have wept so . . .

JASON I never saw her cry. Medea didn't cry. And the only time she ever smiled was the day she said she'd come with me.

MELITE But she did, King Jason. She left her house and home and accepted her fate. You were cruel, too, when you were young.

JASON I was young, Melite. And no one ever laughed at me in those days. But I didn't know yet that all of you in the temple held knowledge and that I was asking the impossible of the goddess. And yet nothing was impossible for us dragon slayers and lords of the golden glitter? You do bad things to become great, to be a god.

MELITE Why were your victims always women?

JASON Sweet little Melite, you're from the temple. You all in the temple must know that a man climbs up there to be god, at least for a day, for an hour, to revel with you as if you were the goddess herself. That man is always imagining he's with her—but then he realizes that he's holding mortal flesh, just a poor woman like you, like all women are. So he becomes enraged—and starts looking everywhere, trying to be god.

MELITE Yet it's good enough for some.

JASON Sure, for someone who's old before his time, or who climbs the hill to get to you. But not before having tried everything else. Not the man who's seen other days. Have you ever heard about the son of Aegeus who went down into Hades to kidnap Persephone—he was the Athenian king who died when he was hurled into the ocean?

MELITE They talk of it in Phalerum. He was a seafarer, like you.

JASON He was practically a god, sweet Melite. And he found his woman across the sea, a woman who, like the sorceress, helped him complete his deadly task. He abandoned her on an island one morning. Then he performed many other feats, other skies, the moon, he had Antiope, savage Amazon. And then Phaedra, light of days, and she killed herself too. Then Helen, daughter of Leda. And others. He ended up trying to wrest Persephone from the jaws of Hades. You know, there was only one woman who didn't love him, who fled Corinth—the child killer, the sorceress.

MELITE But you, my king, remember her. You're better than that other king. And after that, you stopped making people cry.

JASON In Corinth I've learned not to be a god. And I met you, Melite.

MELITE What am I, Jason?

JASON A lady of the seas who comes down from the temple when the old man calls her. And you are also the goddess.

MELITE I serve her.

JASON The island in the west that bears your name is a great sanctuary to the goddess. Right?

MELITE It's a little name, given to me as a joke. Sometimes I do think about beautiful names—of the sorceresses and unhappy women who wept for men like you . . .

JASON Megara Iole Auge Hippolyta Omphale Deianira . . . Do you know who they made cry?

MELITE Oh, well, he was a god. And now he lives among the gods.

JASON So it is said. Poor Heracles. He was with us too. I don't envy him.

IN THE VINEYARD

Leucothea & Ariadne

Ariadne—abandoned by Theseus after his adventure in the labyrinth on the island of Naxos, rescued by Dionysus on his way back from India, and ending up among the constellations in the sky.

LEUCOTHEA Ariadne, will you be crying for much longer?

ARIADNE Where did you come from?

LEUCOTHEA From the sea, like you. So, have you had enough crying now?

ARIADNE I'm not alone anymore.

LEUCOTHEA I had thought that mortal women only cried when someone was listening.

ARIADNE You're rather mean for a nymph.

LEUCOTHEA Well then, so he's left too? Why do you think he left you?

ARIADNE You still haven't told me who you are.

LEUCOTHEA I'm the woman who did what you won't. I tried to drown myself in the sea. My name was Ino and a goddess saved me. Now I'm the nymph of this island.

ARIADNE What do you want from me?

LEUCOTHEA The way you're talking to me, it seems like you already know. I've come to tell you that your beloved boyfriend, with the fancy words and the purple curls, is gone forever. He left you here. Your last memory of him will be the black sails of his ship disappearing in the distance. You can run, wail, argue, but it's over.

ARIADNE Did they leave you too? Is that why you tried to kill yourself?

LEUCOTHEA This isn't about me. And you're not worthy of this conversation. You're ridiculous and stubborn.

ARIADNE Listen here, you water nymph, whatever you have to tell me—I don't know. You're not saying much and if I wanted to kill myself, I know how to do it all by myself.

LEUCOTHEA You don't know anguish, you nitwit. Believe me.

ARIADNE So why did you come here to tell me that?

LEUCOTHEA Why do you think he left you?

ARIADNE Oh stop it, nymph . . .

LEUCOTHEA There, there, go on and cry. At least it's easier that way. No use talking. Flush out the stupidity, the vanity. Then your pain will be revealed for what it is. But until your heart breaks, until you're howling like a bitch and want to end it all in the sea like some average man—you can't say that you know anything about pain.

ARIADNE My heart . . . it's already broken . . .

LEUCOTHEA Don't talk now, just cry . . . You don't know anything yet. There is more to come for you.

ARIADNE What's your name now, nymph?

LEUCOTHEA Leucothea. Do you get it, Ariadne, those black sails are gone forever. This love has ended.

ARIADNE It's my life that's ended.

LEUCOTHEA You're ridiculous. There's more to come. Do you not venerate gods where you come from?

ARIADNE Which god will bring the ship back to me?

LEUCOTHEA I'm asking which gods you have.

ARIADNE There's a mountain back home that inspired fear, even for the sailors on that ship. The greatest gods were born there. We worshipped them. I've already invoked all of them, but no one has come to help me. What will become of me? Can you tell me.

LEUCOTHEA Why would you wait for gods?

ARIADNE I'm not waiting for anything anymore.

LEUCOTHEA So then listen. Someone's coming.

ARIADNE What do you mean?

LEUCOTHEA If I'm talking to you, someone's making a move.

ARIADNE But you're just a nymph.

LEUCOTHEA Nymphs can announce great gods.

ARIADNE Who, Leucothea? Who would do that?

LEUCOTHEA Are you thinking of the god or of the good-looking boy?

ARIADNE I don't know. What do you mean? I bow down to the gods.

LEUCOTHEA So you get it. He's a new god. He's the youngest of them. He saw you and likes you. They call him Dionysus.

ARIADNE I never heard of him.

LEUCOTHEA He was born in Thebes and he wanders the world. He's a joyous god. Everyone cheers him and follows him.

ARIADNE Is he powerful?

LEUCOTHEA He laughs when he kills. Bulls and tigers walk with him. His life is a party, and he likes it that way.

ARIADNE How did he see me?

LEUCOTHEA Who knows. Were you ever in a vineyard on the coast at the sleepy hour when the ground gives off fragrance? That rough, sticky smell, like a cross between a fig and a pine? When the grapes are ripe and the air is heavy with must? Have you ever watched a pomegranate flower and make fruit? That's where Dionysus rules, in the shadow of vines, in pine groves and on farms.

ARIADNE Is there any place so isolated the gods can't see us?

LEUCOTHEA My dear, the gods are the place, are solitude, are the time passing. Dionysus will come and you'll feel like you're being swept away by a huge gust of wind, like the ones that move through the furrows in fields and through vineyards.

ARIADNE When is he coming?

LEUCOTHEA I am announcing him. That's why the boat took off.

ARIADNE Who told you?

LEUCOTHEA I'm from Thebes, Ariadne. His mother is my sister.

ARIADNE Back home they said that gods were born on Ida. No mortal ever climbed past the highest trees. Even the shadow the mountain casts inspires fear. How can I believe what you're saying?

LEUCOTHEA You have been very daring, little one. Wasn't the one with the purple curls a god to you?

ARIADNE I saved that god's life. What was I thinking?

LEUCOTHEA Oh, so many things. You were trembling and hurting. You thought about dying. You've discovered what reawakening feels like. Now you're all alone waiting for a god.

ARIADNE What's he like? Is he very cruel?

LEUCOTHEA They're all cruel. What does that mean anyway? Divinity is cruel. It destroys anything that resists it. In order to wake up stronger, you need to give in to sleep. No god ever regrets anything.

ARIADNE The Theban, this god of yours . . . you said that he kills laughing?

LEUCOTHEA He kills his resisters. He annihilates them. But he's not more unforgiving than the others. Smiling is like breathing for him.

ARIADNE He's not that different from a mortal.

LEUCOTHEA My child, this is another reawakening. It will be like loving a place, a stream of water, an hour of the day. No man is worth as much. Gods endure as long as what made them. For as long as the goats leap through the vineyards and pine groves, you'll like him and he'll like you.

ARIADNE I will die, as all goats do.

LEUCOTHEA There are stars in the vineyard at night too. The god waiting for you is a nocturnal god. Don't be scared.

TINY PEOPLE

Kratos & Bia

Kratos and Bia—Power and Violence—their reward, Hesiod writes, for aiding in the battle against the Titans, was to "have no house apart from Zeus." We all know about the flight of Zeus, and his many stories.

KRATOS He left and now he's down there walking among the humans. He follows the valley road and then lingers in vineyards or along the shore. Sometimes he gets all the way to the gates of a city. You'd never know he's Lord and Father. Every so often I wonder what he wants, what he's looking for. After all that fighting, to get his hands on the world—the countryside, the mountain peaks, and the clouds . . . He could sit up here in peace. But no sir. He walks.

BIA What's so strange about that? When you're the boss, you get to do what you want.

KRATOS So far from the mountain, from us, right? If he's the lord, he owes us, his subjects. He should be pleased the world fears and worships him. But what is he getting from all those tiny people?

BIA They're part of the world too, my dear.

KRATOS I don't know. Something's different from before. Mother said it: "It will come on like a storm and change seasons." This son of the Mountain who rules with a gesture is nothing at all like the old rulers—Night, Earth, the old Sky, or Chaos. You could say the world is divided. There was a time when things happened. Everything had its end, and everything was a living whole. But now there's a law and there's a mind. He made himself immortal and us too. Even the tiny people think about us and know they will die. I understand them up to this point; it's why we defeated the Titans. But he, celestial of the Mountain, who promised us these gifts, is always down there, silly frolicking, living like a man among men—I just don't like it. What do you think, sister?

BIA He wouldn't be king if he couldn't break his own laws. But is he really breaking them?

KRATOS I don't get it, that's a fact. When we moved on the mountains, he smiled like he'd already won. He fought with few words and some nods of his head. He never claimed to be outraged; his enemy was already down, and he kept smiling. That's how he crushed both Titans and men. I liked him then; he was remorseless. There was another time he smiled that way, when he thought of sending Pandora down to punish men for stealing fire. How can someone like that be satisfied with vineyards and cities?

BIA Maybe the woman, Pandora, is not simply a curse. Why shouldn't he amuse himself this way—it was his gift after all?

KRATOS But don't you know what men are? Pitiful things that die. More pitiful than worms or last year's leaves blind to their own decay. But they know that, they repeat it, and they never fail to invoke us, asking for favors or attention, lighting fires, the very same fire they stole away in the hollow of a fennel stalk. And so, with the women, with the offerings, with the chanting and pretty words, they get one of us, an immortal, to walk among them, look at them with kindness, even parent children. Don't you see how calculating it is, the pitiful and brazen cunning? Don't you get why it bothers me so much?

BIA Mother said it, and so did you, the world has changed. The Lord of the mountains didn't start yesterday his mingling with mankind. Maybe you're forgetting when he lived in exile on an island in the middle of the sea, and he died there and was buried there, as happened to gods back then?

KRATOS Those are things we all know.

BIA But it doesn't mean his reach is obsolete. The lords of Chaos are obsolete, that's who; they ruled without law. Before humans, before animals, before stone, there was god. Nothing that happened had a name or a law. We needed god's fugue, the massive sacrilege of his exile among men as a child, a suckling goat, being raised in the mountain forests, speaking words and following the rules of people, knowing the pain of regret and death—all to make the son of Chronos into the good Judge, the immortal and unquiet Mind. You think you helped conquer the Titans? You just said it yourself, he fought as if he'd already won. The reborn child becomes a lord living among men.

KRATOS And so be it. The law was worth it. But what's the compulsion to go back there, now that he's king of all of us?

BIA Brother, brother, brother, can't you see that the world is no longer divine. But that's exactly what's novel and intriguing about it for those descending from the Mountain. The human word, which tastes of suffering and strangulation, which owns the earth, reveals wonders to those willing to listen. The young gods who came up under the rule of Chaos all walk the earth among mortals. Sure, there are some who still feel love for the mountain peaks, the caves, the unruly skies—but they get that from the people who've gotten to the same place, whose voices love to violate silence.

KRATOS If the son of Chronos were only there to walk. If he were there to listen and punish according to the law. But what's persuading him to enjoy it all and allow it to be enjoyed, why steal women and children from those very mortals?

BIA If you met them, you'd understand. They are poor worms but everything about them is unpredictable and out in the open. We know the beast, we know the idol, but no one, not even us, knows the depths of those mortal hearts. There are even those among them who dare challenge destiny. Only by living with them and for them can you know the taste of the world.

KRATOS Or the women, the daughters of Pandora—those beasts?

BIA Women or beasts, they're all the same. What do you think you're saying? They are the richest fruit of mortal life.

KRATOS Does Zeus approach them as beast or god?

BIA You fool, he approaches them like a man. That's all.

THE MYSTERY

Dionysus & Demeter

Everyone likes hearing stories about the initiation rituals in the Eleusinian Mysteries, about which Demeter and Dionysus (and Kore and Pluto) present models of divine immortality. It's less charming to hear about how Demeter is the stalk—bread—and Dionysus is the grape—wine. "Take this and eat . . ."

DIONYSUS These mortals are really amusing. They do things and we know things. I wonder what the days would look like without them. What would we Olympians be? They invoke us with their little voices and give us names.

DEMETER I was here before them, and I can tell you that it was lonely. The earth was forests, snakes, turtles. We were the earth, the air, the water. What could we do? That was when we got into the habit of being eternal.

DIONYSUS Something people can't do.

DEMETER It's true. Everything they touch becomes time. It becomes an action. Waiting and hoping. For them, even dying is something.

DIONYSUS They have this way of naming themselves and things and us—it makes life richer. Like the vineyards they figured out how to plant on these hills. When I first brought the sprout, I never would have thought you could make such a lovely place out of ugly, steep, rocky slopes. It's the same with the crops and the gardens. Anywhere they put in work and words, a rhythm is born, a meaning, a stillness.

DEMETER And the stories they tell about us? I wonder sometimes if I'm really Gaia, Rhea, Cybele, and the Great Mother they say I am. They give us names that reveal ourselves to us. Iacchus, they yank us from the weight of eternal destiny to color us into the days and places where we are.

DIONYSUS To us, you'll always be Deò.

DEMETER Who would have guessed they have such wealth in their poverty? To them, I'm an overgrown and unforgiving mountain, I'm a cloud and a cave, I'm the ruler of lions, crops, and bulls, walled fortresses, ruler of the crib and the tomb, mother of Kore. I owe them everything.

DIONYSUS They're always talking about me too.

DEMETER And shouldn't we help them more, Iacchus, pay them back somehow, be with them during the brief time allowed them?

DIONYSUS You already gave them crops and I gave them grapes. Leave it alone, Deò. What else do they need?

DEMETER I don't know why, but everything that comes from our hands is equivocal. A double-edged dagger. My own Triptolemus barely escaped with his life when he brought the gift of wheat to that Scythian king. I sense you've shed innocent blood too.

DIONYSUS They wouldn't be men if they didn't have sadness. Their life must die. Death is their great wealth, it drives them to work, to remember, to plan ahead. Don't believe, Deò, that their blood is worth more than the grain and wine we feed them with. Blood is dirty and cheap.

DEMETER You're young, Iacchus—you don't know they found us in blood. You run restlessly around the world, and you think death is like some drunken high. But don't think that mortals haven't suffered everything they say about us. How many mortal mothers lost their Kore and never got her back. The highest honor they know how to pay us is bloodshed.

DIONYSUS Is that paying homage, Deò? You know better than I do they used to think killing their victim was like killing us.

DEMETER And were they wrong? That's why I'm saying, they found us in blood. If death is the end and the beginning for them, they had to kill us to see us reborn. They're so unhappy, Iacchus.

DIONYSUS You think? They seem stupid to me. Or maybe not. Seeing that they're so mortal they find sense in life by killing themselves. Each one has to live and die his own story. Think of Icarius . . .

DEMETER Poor Erigone . . .

DIONYSUS Yes, but Icarius got himself killed because he wanted it. Maybe he thought his blood was wine. It was like a madness, the way he harvested and squashed the grapes, how he pruned the vines. That was the first time they saw frothing must on the threshing room floor. They spattered the walls with it, the gardens, the scythes. Even Erigone plunged her hands in it. So why did that stupid old man go out into the fields to make the shepherds drink? Drunk, poisoned, raring, they gutted him over the hedges like a goat and then buried him to make more wine. He knew that would happen and he wanted it. How surprised could his daughter really have been? She'd tasted the wine too. She knew. What other way was there to make the story end, except by hanging herself in the sunshine like grapes on a vine? There's nothing sad about it. The mortals tell stories with blood.

DEMETER And we seem worthy of all this to you? Have you even asked yourself where we would be without them—you know they may get bored of us gods one day. You can see how much you care about this petty blood.

DIONYSUS What do you think we should give them? Whatever it is, they'll make blood of it.

DEMETER There's only one way, and you know it.

DIONYSUS Tell me.

DEMETER To give death meaning.

DIONYSUS What are you saying?

DEMETER Teach them to bless life.

DIONYSUS That would be tempting fate, Deò. They're only mortal.

DEMETER Listen here. Someday they'll come up with this on their own. They'll do it without us, do it through stories. They'll tell of men who conquered death. Some of them have already been in the sky, others go down to hell every six months. One of them fought Death and wrenched a soul from his grasp . . . Think about it. They're going to go it alone. Then we'll go back to being what we were: air, water, and dirt.

DIONYSUS They won't survive longer that way.

DEMETER Silly child, what do you think? Yet dying will have meaning. They'll die to be reborn too, and they won't need us anymore.

DIONYSUS What do you want to do, Deò?

DEMETER Teach them they can match us from down there with their suffering and death. But we will be the ones to tell them. The same way that wheat and grapes sink down into Hades to be born again—that's how we'll teach them that death is new life for them too. We'll give them this story. We'll lead them with this story. Teach them a destiny that cleaves with our own.

DIONYSUS They'll die anyway.

DEMETER They'll die and they'll have conquered death. They will see beyond blood, they'll see the two of us. They'll stop fearing death and won't need to placate it with more spilled blood.

DIONYSUS It could be done, Deò, it could. It will be the story of eternal life. I almost envy them. They won't know destiny and they will be immortal. But I wouldn't count on that stopping the bloodshed.

DEMETER They'll think only of eternity. There's even the risk they'll squander these rich fields.

DIONYSUS For a time. But once the grain and vineyards signify eternal life, you know what humans will see in bread and wine? Flesh and blood, like they do now, like they always do. Flesh and blood will flow, not to placate death, but rather to reach the waiting eternal.

DEMETER It's like you can see the future. How can you say that?

DIONYSUS I've seen the past, Deò. Believe me. But I agree. It will always be a story.

THE FLOOD

Satyr & a wood nymph

Then the Greek flood was the human race's punishment for having lost respect for the gods. And we know that afterward, the earth was repopulated by hurling stones at it.

WOOD NYMPH I do wonder what mortals think of all this water.

SATYR What would they know? They deal with it. Some of them are probably hoping it will bring a better harvest.

WOOD NYMPH At this point the rivers have overflowed, the plants are uprooted. It's raining on water everywhere now.

SATYR They are crowded into the caves and crevices on mountains. They're listening to the rain. They worry about the people left down in the valleys to defend against the water. And they're fooling themselves.

WOOD NYMPH As long as it's night, they can stay deluded. But tomorrow morning, in the harshest daylight, they'll see ocean meeting the sky, and see the mountains have shrunk. They won't go back into the caves. They will look. They will throw a sack over their heads and look.

SATYR You're confusing them with wild animals. Mortals don't understand they're dying and watching death. They need to run, to think, to discuss. The ones that survive will talk to each other.

WOOD NYMPH But there won't be anyone left this time. So, what will they do then?

SATYR I want them here. Once they know they're all condemned, the lot of them, they'll start to celebrate, you'll see. Then, maybe, they'll come looking for us.

WOOD NYMPH So—what does that have to do with us?

SATYR It has plenty to do with us. For them, we're the celebration, we're life. Up to the very end they'll be trying to find life in us.

WOOD NYMPH I don't understand what life we can give them. We don't even know how to die. All we know how to do is look. Look and see. But you're saying they won't look and are unable to accept. What else could they want from us?

SATYR So much, little goat. We're wild animals to them. Animals are born and die, like leaves. If they spot us among the trees, they'll think we're some kind of divinity, and if we run and hide from them that means we're the perpetuation of life in the forest—life that's like theirs but richer and more enduring. I'm telling you they're going to come looking for us. We're their last hope.

WOOD NYMPH With all this water? What will they do then?

SATYR Don't you know what hope is? They'll think that any forest we live in can't be flooded. They will say that all the people, every last one, cannot just disappear, otherwise what was the point of being born, or meeting us? They'll know the great Olympians wanted them dead, but that we, like them, like all small creatures—we are, in the end, life, earth, the truth that matters. The seasons of their lives will meld into celebration, and we are the celebrated.

WOOD NYMPH It's convenient. Hope for them and destiny for us. But it's ridiculous.

SATYR Not very. Something will save them.

WOOD NYMPH And who angered the great gods in the first place? Who caused all this mayhem? Even the sun is hiding its face. I think it's their turn. It serves them right.

SATYR Go on, little goat, is that what you really believe? Don't you think that if they really had violated life, life would be punishment enough—without the Olympians needing to flood us out too? If there was a violation, believe me, it wasn't them.

WOOD NYMPH Meanwhile, they get to die. What will they think tomorrow when they realize what's happening?

SATYR Listen to the rushing water, little one. We'll be underwater tomorrow too. You love to watch but you'll see heinous things. At least we can't die.

WOOD NYMPH I don't know. Sometimes, I ask myself what it means to die. That's the only thing we're really missing. We know everything but we don't know this one simple thing. I'd like to try it and then wake up, you know.

SATYR Listen to her. That's what dying actually is—not knowing you're dead. That's what this flood is: so many dying that there's no one left to know. That's why they'll come looking for us and asking us to save them and they'll want to be like us, like plants, like stones, like non-sentient things that are pure destiny. That's how they'll save themselves. When the waters recede, the rocks and trees emerge like before. That's all the mortals want—for it to go back to how it was.

WOOD NYMPH Odd people. They treat both destiny and the future as if it were the past.

SATYR That's what hope means. To give destiny the name of a memory.

WOOD NYMPH Do you really believe they'll turn into trees and rocks?

SATYR Those mortals know how to tell stories. In the future they'll live according to the terror of tonight and tomorrow, and how it shapes their imagination. They will become wild animals and stones and plants. They will be gods. They will dare to kill off the gods just to see them reborn. They'll turn this past into an escape from death. Hope and destiny—that's all there is.

WOOD NYMPH When it's like this, I don't know how to sympathize. It must be nice to do everything yourself on a whim.

SATYR It is nice. But don't assume they know they're being whimsical. They'll stumble blindly toward some extraordinary salvation after they've been seized and squashed by fate. There's no time to enjoy whimsy. Yes, they know only personal retribution.

WOOD NYMPH At least this flood shows them what's a game and what's celebration. What whim we immortals know is imposed on us by destiny—why can't they learn how to live an eternal moment in all their torment? Why don't they comprehend how precious their temporariness makes them?

SATYR One can't have everything, little one. Those of us who know don't have preferences. The ones who live unpredictable, unique moments don't see the value. They want our eternity. That's how the world is.

WOOD NYMPH By tomorrow they'll know something too. And the rocks and earth emerging back into the light won't be living by hope alone or agony alone. You'll see, the next world will have something divine even in its most intransient mortals.

SATYR If that's God's plan, little goat. I'd like that too.

THE MUSES

Mnemosyne & Hesiod

What a topic. This writer is all too aware of how much gets dared at a glimpse of even one spirit of the nine, or three times three, just three, even two, the Muses and Graces. And yet this writer believes in them, like so many other things. In the world of our story, the mothers are often their daughters, and vice versa. There's even proof. Do we need proof? We should just invite readers to take pleasure in the fact that according to the Greeks, supplications to imagination and memory were almost always held on mountaintops—rather hilltops—and reinvigorated along the way as people migrated down the peninsula.

MNEMOSYNE So, in the end, you're not happy.

HESIOD I can tell you that if I think of something from the past, a time that has ended, I feel like I've been there. But it's different living it. Tasks and things bore me, as if I were a drunk. So then I stop what I'm doing and come up here, to the mountain. And then here, I think back on it all and I feel like I'm happy again.

MNEMOSYNE That's the way it'll always be.

HESIOD You know all the names—which one applies to this condition I'm feeling?

MNEMOSYNE You can use my name, or yours.

HESIOD My name is a human name, Melete, it's empty. But what do you want to be called? There's a different word each time you're invoked. You're like the mother whose name gets lost over the years. They talk about you a lot in the houses and on the paths down at the base of the mountain. It's said you came from Thrace or Thessaly, where the mountains are much more formidable, with snowcaps, black trees, and monsters. And they called you Muse. Then there's Calliope and Cleo. Which name is the real one?

MNEMOSYNE That actually is where I'm from. And I have a lot of names. I'll get more along the way . . . Aglaia, Hegemon, Faenna, whatever the locals come up with.

HESIOD So you get bored too, and that's what keeps you moving on? Does that mean you're not a goddess?

MNEMOSYNE Neither boredom nor goddess, my dear. Today I like Helicon, this mountain, maybe because you're always here. I love being around people—but a little off to the side. I'm not looking for someone particular and I'll talk to anyone who knows how to talk.

HESIOD I don't know how to talk, Melete. And I feel as if I know anything only when I'm with you. The past is in your voice, in all your names, in every season I remember.

MNEMOSYNE In Thessaly my name was Mneme.

HESIOD There are some who say you're old, decrepit, and hard, like a turtle. Others say you're an unripe nymph, like a rosebud or a cloud . . .

MNEMOSYNE What do you think?

HESIOD I don't know. You're Calliope and you are Mneme. You have the voice and gaze of an immortal. You're like a hill or stream—there's no asking how old or young they are, because they have no time. They just are. That's all we know.

MNEMOSYNE My dear, you just are too, but for you, existence means dissatisfaction and boredom. What do you imagine life is like for an immortal?

HESIOD I don't imagine it, Melete, I venerate it the best I am able, with a pure heart.

MNEMOSYNE Go on. I like this.

HESIOD I've said everything.

MNEMOSYNE I know you men, you're not very forthcoming.

HESIOD All we can do before a god is drop to our knees.

MNEMOSYNE Don't worry about the gods. I existed before the gods. You can talk to me. People tell me everything. You can worship us if that's what you want, but can you tell me what you imagine my life is like.

HESIOD How could I know that? I've never been deemed worthy to share the bed of a goddess.

MNEMOSYNE You fool, there are seasons and that one is over.

HESIOD I know only the land I've worked.

MNEMOSYNE You are proud, shepherd. You've got a mortal's pride. But you're destined to know more. Tell me why you think you're happy when you're talking to me?

HESIOD I can answer you that. The things you say don't bore me as much as what happens every day. You give names to things and that makes them different, inconceivable and yet also sweet and familiar like a voice that's kept silent for too long. Or like suddenly seeing your reflection in the water and saying, "Who is that man?"

MNEMOSYNE Have you ever, dear man, seen a plant, or stone, or gesture and felt the same passion?

HESIOD It's happened.

MNEMOSYNE And have you ever figured out why?

HESIOD It's but a moment, Melete. How can I grasp it?

MNEMOSYNE Haven't you ever wondered why a given moment, just like so many other moments past, would grant you a flash of happiness, make you happy like a god? You were looking at the olive tree, the same olive tree on the same trail you've walked every day for years, and then one day your exasperation lifts, you caress that old trunk with your eyes, almost as if you were looking at a long-lost friend who utters the very word your heart's been waiting for.

Maybe another time it's the glance of someone walking past. Or the rain that doesn't let up for days. The shattering call of a bird. Or a cloud you've seen before. Time stops for a moment and the most ordinary thing seizes your heart as if there were no before or after. Haven't you ever wondered why?

HESIOD You just said it yourself. The moment turns the thing into a memory, a model.

MNEMOSYNE Can't you imagine an existence made up entirely of these moments?

HESIOD I can think it, yes.

MNEMOSYNE So you do know how I live.

HESIOD I believe you, Melete, because you carry everything in your eyes. The name Euterpe, which many people call you, doesn't surprise me anymore. But mortal moments aren't a whole life. If I were to want to repeat them, they'd lose their bloom. And then the boredom comes back.

MNEMOSYNE And yet you said that moment is a memory. What is a memory if not repeating passion? Do you get it?

HESIOD What do you mean?

MNEMOSYNE I mean that you do know what immortal life is like.

HESIOD It's difficult to disagree when I'm talking to you. You've seen everything from the beginning. You're the olive tree, the glance, the cloud. You give it a name, and it lasts forever.

MNEMOSYNE I see you up here every day, Hesiod. There were others before you who I'd see in these mountains, on the parched rivers of Thrace or Pieria. But I like you more than them. You know immortal things are close at hand.

HESIOD It's not a difficult thing to know. It's harder to grasp.

MNEMOSYNE This is what you must live for, Hesiod. This is what having a pure heart means.

HESIOD Listening to you, of course. But a man's life unfolds down there, in the houses, in the fields. At the hearth, in bed. And with each new day, you face the same effort and the same incompleteness. It's boredom to the end, Melete. A storm reinvigorates the fields—neither death nor terrible pain is discouraging. But the effort is interminable, the effort to stay alive from one moment to the next—when you hear about the wickedness of others, petty evil, all as bothersome as flies in summer. This is how living cripples you, Melete.

MNEMOSYNE I come from the most desolate places, foggy, lifeless ravines, and even there life is open. Here among the olive trees, under this sky, you are ignorant of that fate. Have you ever heard about the swamp of Boibe?

HESIOD No.

MNEMOSYNE It's a land of fog and mud and reeds—like the beginning of time, a burbling silence. Monsters and gods were birthed there from excrement and blood. The people of Thessaly hardly ever speak of it. It's unchanged by time and seasons. No voice can reach it.

HESIOD And yet you speak of it, Melete, and you've turned it into a divine fate. Your voice reached there. Now, it's an awful and sacred place. The olive trees and the skies of Helicon are not everything in life.

MNEMOSYNE But neither is the boredom. Neither is going home. Can't you understand that people, all people, are born from the blood of that swamp? The sacred and divine are with even you, in your bed, in the fields, at the hearth. Every move you make mimics a divine one. Day and night, there's not a single one of your moments, not even the most useless, that doesn't emerge from the silence of origins.

HESIOD I can never disagree with what you say, Melete. Worshipping you will have to be enough.

MNEMOSYNE There's another way, my dear.

HESIOD Which is?

MNEMOSYNE Try telling the mortals everything you know.

THE GODS

The mountain is uncultivated, my friend. There are patches of snow on last winter's red grass. It looks like the hide of a Centaur. That's what all these high places are like. It takes nothing for land to revert to how it was when all of this happened.

I wonder if they really saw them.

Who knows? Of course, they saw them. They said their names and nothing more—and that is the whole difference between fairy tale and reality, "It was this guy or that other guy," "He did this, he said that." The truthful one makes due. Wouldn't even suspect they might not believe him. We're the liars, because even though we never saw those things, we are absolutely sure we know about the Centaur's hide, or the color of the grapes in Icarus's vineyard.

All you need is a hill, a peak, a coast—a solitary place, and when you lift your eyes, they pause on the sky. The unbelievable pungency of whatever is in the air touches your heart again today. I, for one, believe that the silhouettes of trees or rocks against the sky were gods from the very beginning.

It hasn't all been on mountains.

Sure. First there were the voices of the earth—aquifers, roots, snakes. If the demon brings the earth and sky together, then the demon must emerge from the dark soil into the light.

I don't know. Those people knew too many things. With the simplest name, they could tell the story of a cloud, the forest, the fates. We barely know what they certainly saw. They had neither the time nor the inclination to get lost in dreams. They saw terrible, unbelievable things and weren't at all shocked. They knew what it was. If they were liars, then you're losing your mind when you say, "It's morning" or "Looks like rain."

Sure, they had names. I often wonder which came first, the names or the things.

Believe me, it was at the same time. And it was here, in these lonely, dry places. Is it so surprising they came up here? What else would they have been looking for if not to meet gods?

Who can say why they stopped here. But there's an emptiness about all abandoned places, a waiting.

There's nothing else to think about up here. These places have had names forever. All that's left is grass under the sky, and yet there's a whisper in the wind that calls to mind the memory of a storm blustering through the forest. There's neither emptiness nor waiting. That which has been is forever.

They're dead and buried though. And now these places are the way they were before. I'll grant what they said was true. But what else is there? You have to admit there are no gods left to encounter along this path. When I say "It's morning" or "Looks like rain," I'm not talking about them.

It's what we talked about last night. Yesterday you were talking about the summer and that longing to breathe in warm evening air. Other times you've held forth about mankind, the people you've been with, what you used to like, unexpected encounters. All things that once were. I can assure you, I listened to you the way I listen to those ancient names repeating in my head. When you talk about what you know, I don't answer, "What else is there?" Or ask whether words or things came first. I live with you and with you I feel alive.

It's not easy to live as if what happened in the past was true. Yesterday when the fog descended on us in the fallow fields and some rocks rolled down the hill to stop at our feet, we didn't think about divinity or a wondrous encounter; we thought about the night and the hares running everywhere. Who we are and what we believe emerges in discomfort, in the reckless hour.

It will be nice to talk with friends about that night and the hares when we're back home. Yet we have to smile at fear, the thought of how grueling it must have been for people living in a time when everything they touched was mortal. People for whom the air was full of nighttime terrors, mystical threats, scary memories. Even just bad weather or an earthquake. And if this unease was real, as it is indisputable, their courage was also real, and hope was, and the lovely discovery that a promise to meet up has power. I, for one, never get tired of hearing them talk about their dread of the night and what they hoped for.

And do you believe in monsters, believe in animal people, in living stones, divine smiles, and in words that annihilate?

I believe in that which every person has hoped for and endured. If there was a time when they climbed these rocky heights or searched for deadly swamps under the sky, it was because they could find something there we know nothing about. It wasn't bread or pleasure or precious health. We know where those things are. Not here. Those of us who live far away, near the ocean or plains, there's another thing we've lost.

Go on, say it. The thing.

You already know. Those encounters.

archipelago books
is a non-profit publisher devoted to
promoting cross-cultural exchange through innovative
classic and contemporary international literature
archipelagobooks.org

elsewhere editions
translates luminous picture books from around the world
elsewhereeditions.org